"What would it take to make you happy, Katie?"

She bit her lip and gazed at the floor. She said, "That's a hard question to answer. I'm not sure I know."

"What's so hard about it?" Ross asked. "You were miserable before. You must know what it would take to turn that around."

She smiled at him then, a slow, teasing smile that had the warmth of a summer sun. "There are degrees of happiness. A rainbow can make you feel good for a minute. A movie can make you laugh for a couple of hours. A child's hug can give you an instant's joy." Her expression had turned dreamy, and he wondered what she was thinking.

"What else, Katie?" His voice was hoarse as he felt the tension between them thrum with a sudden awareness. It was an exquisitely sweet tension that had been building for days now, maybe longer.

"A kiss," she said, her gaze meeting his boldly...

Sherryl Woods

Sherryl Woods has been a journalist, a television critic, a travel editor, and the coordinator of an employee program at a university medical center in Miami. She's climbed endless steps in an assortment of European castles, bounced over rural Jamaican roads on a motorcycle, and negotiated a few mountainous, hairpin curves in this country, all in search of the perfect setting for romance. However, she's found that the location doesn't matter a bit if the hero by your side is intelligent, funny, sensual and, most of all, sensitive.

Other Second Chance at Love books by
Sherryl Woods

Dear Reader:

We're pleased to announce that the winner of our "*Gamble* sweepstakes," which we told you about in our August 1987 letter, is Mrs. Mary Koenig of Phoenix, Arizona. Mrs. Koenig tells us she's been reading Second Chance at Love romances since we began publishing the series in 1981, and her favorite authors include Carole Buck, Jackie Leigh, Cait Logan, and Courtney Ryan. We're sending a personally inscribed, autographed copy of the bestselling historical romance *The Gamble* by LaVyrle Spencer to Mrs. Koenig, and also to her romance bookseller, Mr. Joe Canas, assistant manager of the Waldenbooks store at the Thomas Mall in Phoenix. Congratulations, Mrs. Koenig and Mr. Canas!

Sherryl Woods and Jamisan Whitney, the authors of our January releases, will keep you in stitches with their own distinctive brands of humor. The winner of the 1986 *Romantic Times* Reviewer's Choice "Pink Fuzzy" award, for the author most likely to cheer readers on a rainy day, Sherryl's created a rollicking comedy about a heroine whose search for Mr. Right produces delightfully surprising results. And Jamisan, the first winner of *Romantic Times*'s WISH (Women in Search of a Hero) award, wonderfully satisfies your requests for a spin-off from her first, critically acclaimed romance, *Driven to Distraction* (#315).

If you've ever placed or answered a Personals ad—or wanted to—you'll especially enjoy *Prince Charming Replies* (#430) by Sherryl Woods. Single parent Katie Stewart advertises for Prince Charming and arranges to meet the most promising respondents—and then her gorgeous boss, Ross Chandler, unexpectedly begins to court her! The other men in her life pique Ross's jealousy, and yet another suitor appears—a secret admirer who writes Katie ever-so-romantic letters. Suddenly, she's so besieged by men, her head's awhirl ... but her heart recognizes her true Prince Charming. *Prince Charming Replies,* Sherryl's sixth Second Chance at Love novel, offers romantic entertainment at its finest—full of warmth, humor, and as much sparkle as the Hope diamond!

Desire's Destiny (#431), Jamisan Whitney's third Second Chance at Love romance, balances laugh-out-loud comedy and emotional depth as philosopher/truck driver Freddy Rotini loses his heart to historian Johanna Remington on the Oregon Trail. Jamisan's created some hilariously memorable secondary characters, like eccentric Charlie Vishtek, who lost his wagon train to Freddy in a poker game, and Charlie's pretentious son, James. Thor and Andee Engborg, the hero and heroine of Jamisan's first romance, appear here, too. Indeed, Andee gives birth during a dramatic scene in which Johanna confronts and conquers her past, freeing herself from the last obstacle to her love for Freddy.

This month we're offering a particularly outstanding selection of longer fiction for you to read on those snowy and sub-freezing days when a good book seems a godsend. For you Judith Michaels fans, we highly recommend first novel *Mirror, Mirror* by Betsy von Furstenberg, an enthralling story about two half-sisters who experience passion and scandal, jealousy and betrayal, amid the glamor of Venice, Paris, and the Bahamas. Bestselling author Barbara Michaels delivers a tour de force of romantic suspense in *Shattered Silk,* and another of our bestselling authors, Shannon Drake—aka Heather Graham Pozzessere—weaves a fascinating web of desire and danger in 17th-century England in *Ondine.* We're also publishing a new Barbara Cartland novel, *Sapphires in Siam,* and a new giant-size Regency by Elizabeth Mansfield, *A Grand Deception.* We're reissuing Georgette Heyer's Regency *Sprig Muslin,* and Mary Westmacott's novel of romantic intrigue *The Rose and the Yew Tree.* You're probably more familiar with Mary Westmacott's other pen name, Agatha Christie, whose mystery *The Murder at Hazelmoor* we're also reissuing in January. Our other mysteries by women writers include *The Doom Campaign* by award-winning author Mary McMullen, *Enter a Murderer* by the renowned Ngaio Marsh; and Heron Carvic's *Witch Miss Seeton,* the launch book of a delightful series that we're publishing in paperback for the first time—we'll be publishing a new Miss Seeton mystery every three months, and they're sure to appeal to all you devotees of Miss Marple and Miss Silver.

As always, we wish you happy reading!

Sincerely,

Joan Marlow

Joan Marlow, Editor
SECOND CHANCE AT LOVE
The Berkley Publishing Group
200 Madison Avenue
New York, NY 10016

SECOND CHANCE AT LOVE™

SHERRYL WOODS
PRINCE CHARMING REPLIES

B
BERKLEY BOOKS, NEW YORK

First edition published January 1988

ISBN: 0-425-10604-7

Second Chance at Love books are published by
The Berkley Publishing Group
200 Madison Avenue, New York, NY 10016

Printed in the United States of America

10 9 8 7 6 5 4 3 2 1

PRINCE CHARMING
REPLIES

PROLOGUE

"COME ON, KATIE, try it! What have you got to lose?"

Stunned, Katie Stewart stared at her best friend, Jennifer Gleason, as if she'd suddenly done a personality switch as dramatic as Dr. Jekyll's and Mr. Hyde's. Where was the logic she'd always counted on from Jennifer? Where was the conservative, think-it-through-before-you-act approach to life?

"I thought you were supposed to be so sensible. For years my mother pleaded with me to be more like you," she replied, as confusing thoughts whirled around in her head. She shook her head adamantly. "Fifteen years ago, I could have done it." She hesitated. "Maybe. Now, it's absurd. I'm a mother. I have a responsibility to demonstrate good judgment. I'm thirty-four years old."

"All the more reason to do it," chimed in Maggie Kincaid. "You're not getting any younger. You don't

1

want to be alone forever. If we were single, you can bet Jennifer and I would do it."

"Here," Jennifer urged. "Have some more champagne. Just imagine the possibilities."

"If I have any more champagne, I'll have nightmares about the possibilities." Katie eyed her friends warily. "Are you two trying to get me drunk so I won't be able to think clearly?"

Jennifer and Maggie exchanged slightly guilty glances, then admitted practically in unison, "Well, it would be a whole lot better if you stopped thinking and worrying and just *did* it."

Katie took a long, slow gulp of the outrageously expensive, delightfully bubbly imported champagne her two friends had brought over to help her get through the first anniversary of her divorce. They'd been afraid she'd be depressed. Obviously, they'd envisioned her drowning her sorrows with a quart of chocolate-chocolate-chip ice cream, clogging her arteries with cholesterol in some sort of a slow suicide attempt.

Actually, she'd never felt better in her life. For the first time ever, she felt she was in control of her own destiny—or she had until Jennifer and Maggie had started plying her with champagne.

The year following the breakup of her marriage had not been a picnic by any means, but she'd managed. Oh, there'd been occasional pints of ice cream to chase away the blues, but she'd been too frantically busy to indulge in self-pitying binges often. With grim determination, she had marched out just a few weeks after the divorce and gotten herself a surprisingly responsible job for a woman with such limited practical skills. She'd also learned to fix the garbage disposal, mow the lawn, change the spark plugs in the car, and still kept her ten-year-old daughter, Lisa, in reasonably neat clothes and on time for school.

On one riotous occasion, she had even stemmed a flood in the kitchen by poking her finger in the broken pipe and yelling her head off until Lisa had finally heard her over the roar of the stereo, raced in, found the cutoff valve, and dialed the number of an all-night plumber. Unfortunately, his task had been somewhat complicated by the fact that her finger had swollen and was solidly stuck in the pipe. It had required first-class surgical skill to extricate it, and the plumber's already astronomical rates had been adjusted accordingly. It had set her budget back by a month.

At any rate, as she saw it, tonight was not an occasion for depression but cause for celebration. She'd survived having Paul Stewart, the only man with whom she'd ever been involved, walk out on her after twelve years of marriage, and she was damn proud of the things she'd accomplished. That did not mean, however, that she was ready for a new relationship, which was exactly what Jennifer and Maggie were prodding her to go for.

"Even if I were ready to start dating—and I'm not saying that I am—I'm not about to place an ad in the newspaper. Finding a man is not like advertising for a used piano, for heaven's sake. You can't buy romance with four lines of type in the classifieds. These things are supposed to happen naturally."

"Have you met a single man this entire last year that you wanted to go out with?" Jennifer demanded.

"Well, no," Katie admitted. An image of her boss flitted through her mind, warmed her blood, and then just as quickly vanished. "Not exactly."

"And not one of your friends has a long list of eligible bachelors to trot out for your inspection, right?"

"No."

"Are you willing to start hanging around singles' bars?"

Katie's expression was suitably horrified. "Of course not. I saw *Looking for Mr. Goodbar*."

"There," Jennifer said triumphantly. "Then you have to try this. Put an ad in the personals column. We've been studying them for the last few weeks. Some of them are a lot of fun. Perfectly respectable people put in ads. Lawyers, doctors, professors. Really, what could happen with some stodgy old professor?"

"Why don't we compromise? Maybe I could just answer an ad."

"No. Bad idea," Maggie said. "You want to be in charge here. Stop worrying so much. What's the worst thing that could happen? Maybe you wouldn't get any answers. It might be humiliating, but you wouldn't die from it."

Katie was still shaking her head. "There is also the chance that I could pick out some homicidal maniac and wind up at the bottom of Puget Sound. Did you two ever think about that?"

"Just don't get in a boat with anybody," Maggie suggested helpfully. Katie glared at her, but Maggie and Jennifer just stared back expectantly. They were not the least bit daunted by her reluctance to go along with them. In fact, they seemed perfectly ready to sit here all night if they had to, until she agreed to their harebrained scheme.

"I'll think about it," she finally conceded with a tiny sigh.

"No," Jennifer said firmly, in the same no-

nonsense way she talked to her kids, one of whom happened to be Lisa's very best friend. "Don't think about it. Let's write your ad right now and mail it in before you can change your mind."

"I haven't even made up my mind," Katie reminded her tartly. In fact, there seemed to be a strange buzzing in her head. It was either the champagne or her good sense trying to warn her that she was about to do something utterly foolish.

At the same time, a shiver of anticipation played along her spine as she toyed with the idea of being able to anonymously pick and choose from among a whole selection of sexy, intriguing bachelors. It was sort of like the old TV show, *The Dating Game*, played out in the privacy of your living room. The idea blossomed into a more and more tantalizing prospect. A nineteen-year-old Katie Stewart definitely would have done it. That Katie had been a risk-taker. But at thirty-four? She had to admit it was still awfully tempting.

Apparently, some of that excitement was putting in an impudent appearance on her face. She always had been a lousy poker player.

"But you're going to," Jennifer said confidently, reading her expression with the unerring accuracy of a longtime friend. "Where's your notepaper?"

Katie had learned a certain amount of independence in the last year, but she'd never been able to withstand the whirlwind effects of Hurricane Jennifer once she'd gotten an idea into her head. Jennifer would find the paper, if she had to turn the house upside down. It was easier just to tell her. "In the desk."

Five minutes later, the three of them were sitting at the dining room table composing an ad to lure the man of Katie's dreams out of hiding and into her arms.

"Let's see now. What are your best characteristics?"

"I'm housebroken," Katie said, giggling softly as she downed the last of her glass of champagne in an effort to get into the spirit of things. The whole plan still struck her as being slightly absurd. Women shouldn't go around advertising for men, especially not women with very wise ten-year-old daughters who needed to have an example set for them. Lisa would think she'd gone 'round the bend.

What the hell? the impudent side of her nature countered. All kids Lisa's age thought their parents were heading 'round the bend for one reason or another.

Jennifer scowled at her facetious comment. "We want someone sexy and exciting to answer this ad, not someone who's looking for a pet. That was Paul's problem. He kept you chained to this house like some sort of glorified servant." She pursed her lips thoughtfully, then began furiously scribbling notes. Katie couldn't resist peeking over her shoulder.

Energetic. Lively. Redhead. Witty. Sensitive. Intelligent. Athletic.

Athletic?

"I'm not athletic," Katie protested.

"But men like women who are into sports."

"Do you want me to build this relationship on a lie? The most athletic thing I do all day is bend over to pull on my panty hose. Unless the conditions are exactly right, I can't even sit through half of a Seahawks game."

"What about canoeing? You and Paul used to go all the time. I thought you loved it."

"He made me go. In fact, I'm not so sure he wasn't trying to drown me to save on future alimony."

"Okay, I'll scratch athletic. Anything else?"

"I make a great peanut-butter-and-jelly sandwich."

"Katie, you're not taking this seriously."

"Oh, yes, I am," she insisted. "I want him to know the full range of my culinary skills before we get involved. If he expects beef Wellington, I'll be in trouble."

"If he wants beef Wellington, he can take you out and order it," Maggie said, pouring the last of the champagne into the three crystal wineglasses they'd supplied along with the champagne. "I mean, we're looking for a high-class sort of guy here, someone who'll shower you with diamonds and furs and take you on fantastic trips."

Maggie sighed with envy, and Katie realized that she, at least, was planning to live vicariously through every minute of this idiotic adventure.

"I'm not a high-class sort of woman," Katie argued. "I drink my soft drinks straight from the can. I wear flannel nightgowns."

"That has to change," Jennifer noted. "We'll go shopping tomorrow."

"But I like flannel nightgowns. I also like nice, down-to-earth, normal men." At nineteen, though, even with Paul's engagement ring on her finger, she'd dreamed of silk gowns and dashing international race-car drivers.

"Katie, we are going to find you someone special, not some dud who'll bore you for the rest of your days," Jennifer countered. "Surely in all of Seattle there's a man like that."

"Of course, there is," Katie agreed. "He's just married to an exciting, sexy woman."

"Dammit all, Katie Stewart, stop putting yourself down!" Maggie flared. "You have a gorgeous face—"

"I learned how to use makeup."

Maggie kept right on going. "—cobalt blue eyes that ought to be outlawed—"

"Which are so nearsighted I can hardly pick my own daughter out of a crowd."

"—and shiny, naturally curly hair that makes me want to shave my head and buy a wig."

"I'd give anything to have long, silky blond hair like yours," Katie said wistfully. "I've always felt like Little Orphan Annie."

"Stop it right this minute!" Maggie clamped her hands over her ears. "I will not listen to another one of your self-deprecating slurs."

"I am not putting myself down. I'm just not getting my hopes up."

"Will you two stop bickering and concentrate?" Jennifer ordered. "We've figured out some of the things we can say about Katie. Now we need to decide what we want the man to be like."

Katie's eyes lit up with a wicked sapphire sparkle. "I thought we were going for a combination of George Hamilton and Indiana Jones," she said hopefully.

"Good idea," Maggie enthused. "That's exactly what you need."

Katie's face fell. "But I was kidding."

"Nope," Jennifer concurred. "Maggie's right. We want someone suave, adventurous, intelligent, and emotionally secure."

"That may take several men. I don't think they

come packaged that way except in the movies," Katie said dryly.

"Well, we're going to shoot for the top. Now, how does this sound?" Jennifer asked, reading what she'd written. "'Feisty, independent redhead with varied interests seeks sincere, intelligent man, thirty-five to forty-five, with zany sense of humor and adventurous spirit to sweep her off her feet. Only Prince Charming need reply.'"

"Why thirty-five to forty-five?" Maggie asked. "What's wrong with a younger man?"

"I don't want to raise another child," Katie said. "I already have Lisa."

"So the ad stands," Jennifer said. Katie could tell from the satisfaction in her voice that it was a statement, not a question, so she didn't even bother to argue. She just watched as Jennifer addressed an envelope to the newspaper. When she began filling out a check, though, Katie stopped her.

"Wait a minute. You're not paying for this."

"Yes, I am. It's my anniversary-of-your-divorce present."

Katie moaned and shook her head. "Don't let anyone in the greeting-card industry hear you say that. They'll have appropriate cards on the market in a month."

Jennifer scowled back at her and tucked the envelope into her purse.

"Give me the envelope," Katie demanded, reaching for it. "I'll mail it in the morning, if I haven't come to my senses by then."

Jennifer put her purse behind her back. "I'll mail it tonight, just to save you from yourself. Come on, Maggie. Let's go, before she tries to hold me down and steal the letter back from me."

"Please, you two. Can't we wait until morning? I'm having second thoughts already."

"You never stopped having second thoughts," Jennifer noted, kissing her on the cheek. "'Night, sweetie. Pleasant dreams."

Maggie gave her a hug. "I can hardly wait until the first batch of mail rolls in. You're going to have the time of your life."

"I'm going to have my head examined," Katie muttered, as she watched the two of them walk away with her future tucked in Jennifer's purse. There was just the slightest slur to her words and a spinning in her head.

"First thing in the morning," she amended.

CHAPTER ONE

Dear Box 7982,

I would have sent roses, but I was afraid they'd wilt before you got them. It's hard to be Prince Charming when you're dealing with a box number. Maybe we could meet and you could see for yourself. I'm tall, dark, and handsome, just like the fairy tales require. I'm also a divorced father of two, thirty-eight, with no incredibly bad habits, despite what my ex-wife might want to tell you. Give me a call at the number below and we can see what else we have in common.

—*Jason*

KATIE SAT AT her desk holding the letter in one hand and a mug of steaming black coffee in the other. Jason. Nice name. She'd never known anyone

11

named Jason before. And he sounded like he might be a lot of fun. She looked at the phone number, then at the batch of unopened mail still scattered across the top of the desk, and shook her head in amazement.

She'd never expected this many responses, especially right away. These men must have written the minute they read the paper. She'd had no idea there were so many people looking for companionship and using the personals to find it.

In fact, in the couple of weeks before her ad had finally appeared, she hadn't given it another thought, assuming that nothing would ever come of it. School had just started again, and there had been a flurry of activity buying new clothes for Lisa, along with the right notebooks and enough pens to stock an entire office for a year. Lisa lost pens the way little children lost their mittens.

Suddenly one morning in the middle of the week, before she'd even had time to finish fixing breakfast, the phone had rung and an excited Jennifer had said, "Well, what do you think? Have you read the paper yet?"

"I barely have my eyes open. What happened? Did something important blow up last night? Did two celebrities finally get married before they had a baby? What?"

"Your ad. It was in this week's edition of *The Weekly*. Get the paper today and see what you think."

"I know what I think," she'd said. "I think we were all looped and had taken leave of our senses."

"We'll talk next week after you get your first letters and see if you feel that way then," Jennifer had said with perfect serenity. "Promise you'll call me the minute they arrive."

"I'll call."

Now, on the following Wednesday, with all of this mail lying on her desk like an untouched Christmas stocking filled with possibilities, Katie felt an impudent little flutter of excitement in the pit of her stomach, and her heartbeat quickened. She must be ready to start dating after all. She wondered if all of these men were as charming and witty as Jason seemed to be.

She nibbled nervously at her full lower lip and reached for another letter.

"What's up, Katie?"

Ross Chandler stood in the doorway of Katie's office and watched the play of expressions on her lovely, fragile face. Those wonderful deep blue eyes gazed up at him in surprise, and a flush of embarrassment tinted her cheeks pink. She looked exactly like a china doll, but he knew there was hidden strength in Katie, a determination that had made her overcome her initial sense of inadequacy following her divorce and had turned her into one of the best executive assistants he'd ever had at Chandler Electronics.

He'd hired her on instinct alone, ignoring the fact that her résumé had virtually nothing on it beyond a practically useless college degree in literature and the presidency of the PTA. He'd told himself that being president of the PTA required the same sort of organizational skills he required, but he knew he'd chosen her over other, more qualified candidates simply because he couldn't bear the thought of not hearing her musical voice again. Every day for the past ten months, he'd waited breathlessly for the first time she flicked on the intercom and announced cheerfully that she was at her desk and ready for whatever challenges the day had to offer. Katie's good spirits never seemed to flag, and her willingness to tackle any assignment, large or small, had long ago convinced him he'd found a real treasure.

Fortunately for Chandler Electronics, Katie had more than an upbeat attitude, a lovely face, and a sexy voice that sent shivers down his spine. She'd absorbed everything he'd taught her, and within two months had been able to offer him startling insights on the operation of the company and, more important, into the character of his key competitors. He'd started having her sit in on every important business meeting, not to take notes—he had a secretary for that—but simply to tell him later what vibes she had picked up. More often than not, she was right on target, and frequently she sensed undercurrents that had escaped him completely.

Right now, though, she looked like a flustered teenager, and she was shuffling a huge stack of mail into a little pile and trying to shove it into her briefcase. He grinned at her.

"Don't tell me," he said with an exaggerated moan. "You've been mailing out your résumé all over town, and these are just the first responses."

He was joking, but the possibility that she might actually leave seemed to slow his heartbeat to a halt. He waited expectantly, hoping for one of her bright smiles. She smiled, but it was very wobbly and weak. She looked even more like a schoolgirl caught cheating on an exam.

"Not exactly."

"What then?"

"It's personal, Ross."

Troubled by her uncharacteristic hesitancy, he walked over, sat on the edge of her desk, and gazed intently into her eyes. She blinked and looked away, then began nervously biting her lower lip again. Her hands were trembling, and suddenly he found that he wanted to take them in his and hold them until whatever was bothering her vanished. He'd felt this unfamiliar surge of masculine protectiveness on several occasions before, always around Katie. It had never failed to disconcert him.

"So personal that you can't tell me about it? I thought we were friends. I thought we could discuss anything. If you're having problems..."

"We are friends, but this is... it's not a problem, exactly." She gave her head a quick shake and squared her shoulders. Delectable shoulders, he noted, not for the first time.

"Katie," he began again, forcing his attention back to her obvious dilemma. "Please. Tell me what's wrong."

"Nothing's wrong." His skepticism didn't waver, and she finally blurted out, "Oh, what the hell... they're answers to an ad."

He breathed a sigh of relief. So, it wasn't a crisis after all. "What kind of ad? Are you trying to sell something?"

"In a way."

"What? The house? Is it getting to be too much for you? I know a very good real-estate broker, if you've decided to sell. She could help you find an apartment, too. Something more manageable."

"It's not the house. Lisa and I love it, despite its idiosyncrasies. We have no intention of moving into some cramped little apartment."

"What, then?"

Katie found she was unable to meet his interested gaze. "Myself," she mumbled.

"What on earth . . . ?"

"You know, one of those things in the personals column that runs in *The Weekly.*"

She took a quick peek at his expression. His brown eyes, which a moment before had been warm with compassion, were suddenly sparkling with amusement, and his laughter echoed off the walls. "You're kidding."

Katie glared at him, and his grin wavered. "My God, you're *not* kidding."

"No, I'm not kidding, and what's wrong with it?" she demanded defiantly, wondering why she was suddenly defending something that she'd fought so hard against in the first place. Why wasn't she laughing with Ross? It must be the astonished look on his face, as if he couldn't imagine anyone being desperate enough to put an ad in the paper for a date.

She scowled and added, "A lot of people are doing it."

Of course, she reminded herself, Ross Chandler was not one of them. He had probably never had to advertise for a date in his life. In fact, he probably rarely had to ask for one. Katie had seen the seemingly endless parade of gorgeous, willowy, aggressive women who streamed in and out of his office. Those were not the meetings he invited her to attend, which meant they were entirely personal. Every one of those women probably received long-stemmed roses at least once a week and shared a gourmet meal with him at one of the best restaurants in town, while *she* was sitting at home with Lisa eating spaghetti with sauce from a jar.

It probably wouldn't do at all to imagine what else

those women got from Ross Chandler. He was a very virile-looking man, the sort of man who conjured up visions of a muscular body scantily wrapped in a towel and glistening wet from the shower even when he was wearing a perfectly respectable three-piece suit. Just thinking about it made goose bumps rise all over her.

Right now he was holding out his hand, a strong, very masculine hand flecked with dark hairs. "Let me see."

"No way." She clutched even more tightly the letters she hadn't been able to hide.

"Come on, Katie," he taunted beguilingly. "Let me look at them."

"I haven't even had a chance to read them myself."

"Then we'll read them together. I'll help you pick one out, and we'll have him vetted. I don't much like the idea of your going out with a total stranger." There was a storm of some sort brewing in his eyes.

"You are not going to start doing background checks on my dates, Ross Chandler," she flared indignantly. "I am perfectly capable of taking care of myself."

"When was the last time you went on a date?" he challenged her.

Katie refused to meet his penetrating gaze. She hated it when those dark, knowing eyes of his bored into her. It was as if he could see into her very soul. That look invariably turned her insides to mush.

"I thought so," he said triumphantly. "You haven't been on a date with a new man since you met your husband back in college, right?"

"High school," she muttered.

"My God. It's worse than I thought. Do you have

any idea what men are like out there today? They're unscrupulous vultures who'll take advantage of an innocent like you."

"I was married for twelve years. That hardly qualifies me as an innocent, and surely not all men are like that."

"Oh, yes, they are."

Her blue eyes suddenly twinkled back at him wickedly. "Even you?" she inquired sweetly.

A slow flush of embarrassment rose up from his neck until it reached the rugged features of his face. "Well . . ." he mumbled.

"I handle you okay, don't I?" she continued to taunt.

"Yes, but you and I aren't . . . I mean, we're in the office, not on a date."

"And if we were, would you be just as unscrupulous as you claim all those other men would be?" The thought did the strangest things to her pulse rate.

"Of course not," he said with what sounded to her like self-righteous indignation. "I respect you."

"Don't you suppose I can earn their respect as well?"

He shook his head decisively. "Not on a first date."

"You don't seem to have very much faith in me."

What he had, Ross decided with a sudden pang, was actually a very bad case of jealousy. It startled the living daylights out of him.

"I do have faith in you, but I still think you should let me see those letters."

"Why?"

Why, indeed? "Because I'm a good judge of character."

"So am I. At least that's what you're always telling me. Don't you mean it?"

Touché, he thought. "Of course I mean it. Okay, how about just one letter? The one you like the best. Call it research. Maybe I'll want to answer one of those ads myself one day. I want to see what you women like, what makes one letter stand out from the rest."

Katie's eyes remained sharply skeptical, but she finally reached into her briefcase and handed him the letter signed Jason.

Ross skimmed the note. Damn! The man did have a certain flair. "Are you going to call him?" he demanded.

"I was thinking about it."

"Do it now."

"Why now?" Katie asked.

"If you're going to do it, you may as well do it now."

She sighed, and the hesitant look in her eyes almost did him in. Why on earth was he pushing her to do this? He didn't want her to make that call any more than he wanted to abandon any future Chandler Electronics projects because his chief competitor, Dorian Hayes, beat him into production. She was already reaching for the phone, though.

"Use the speaker phone," he said insistently.

"Why?"

"So I can listen, of course."

"Are you some kind of strange pervert who likes to snoop on other people's private phone conversations?" she taunted lightly, and Ross wondered what she'd say if she knew the truth. He was terrified that she was going to get herself in over her head with someone more dangerous than a weirdo who listened to phone calls.

"Humor me."

Katie finally shrugged in acquiescence. She heard Ross's sigh of relief as she poked the button for the speaker phone, then dialed the number on Jason's letter. When a secretary answered, Katie gulped and then said, "Is Jason in, please? This is Katie Stewart."

"May I tell him what it's regarding?"

Katie's eyes widened. She hadn't expected this. What on earth was she supposed to say—that the man had responded to her ad? It might embarrass him, to say nothing of making her feel like a jerk.

"Actually, it's rather personal," she said at last, hoping that this woman wasn't one of those secretaries for whom that vague response was an open invitation for deeper probing. Suddenly, she heard an indulgent, motherly chuckle on the other end of the line.

"Oh, he's answered another one of those ads, has he? Just a minute, Ms. Stewart."

Katie could still hear the secretary's good-humored laughter as she was put on hold. A few seconds later, a pleasant, deep voice rumbled in her ear.

"So, you're looking for Prince Charming?" he said with amusement. "If you'd asked for him, I'm sure Dora would have put you straight through without giving you such a hard time."

Katie heard what sounded like a strangled, choking sound coming from Ross. She absolutely refused to look into his eyes, though. She just knew she would burst into laughter, and Jason would think he'd written to a middle-aged nut.

"So, Prince Charming, tell me more about yourself," she said in the dignified, reserved voice she generally used with Ross's business associates. It was a tone thoroughly at odds with the suddenly whimsical, light-headed way she was feeling. For the first time in ages, she felt like flirting. She felt wickedly desirable.

"Why don't we discuss everything you wanted to know about me over lunch?" he suggested. "Then we can talk all about *you* over dinner."

Smooth, Katie thought. The man was very smooth. He was obviously used to getting his way with women. Not with her, though. She was about to refuse when an inner voice chided her. *This is why you ran the ad in the first place*, that nagging little person whispered in her ear. *Jennifer and Maggie would never forgive you for not following through*. Besides, Ross was standing there practically daring her to go through with it.

"Let's just start with lunch," she said at last, noting that Ross was now staring out the window with a fierce scowl on his face. She wondered briefly what that was all about, but Jason was suggesting that he pick her up at noon.

"You mean *today?*" she asked in a horrified whisper. She needed time to prepare, to get a complete makeover, to rearrange at least five pounds. She needed a reprieve.

"Why not? Do you already have plans?"

She had a peanut-butter-and-jelly sandwich and an apple in her briefcase—did that count? Probably not. She sighed. "Today would be fine."

"Terrific. I'll pick you up at noon. Just tell me where you are."

Suddenly, Ross was shaking his head and practically jumping up and down to get her attention.

"Excuse me," she murmured into the phone. "Someone just stepped into my office." She flipped off the speaker and put her hand over the receiver. "What on earth is wrong with you?"

"You're not getting into a car with a total stranger," he said adamantly.

She blinked at his harsh tone, started to rebel, and then realized he was absolutely right. She nodded, and started to talk directly into the phone, but Ross was beside her in an instant, turning the speaker back on.

"I'll meet you," she told Jason. "Just pick the place, and I'll be there."

He named a lovely seafood restaurant overlooking the water. "Is that convenient?"

Actually, it was clear across town, but she loved the place. Ross had taken her there to celebrate a business deal a few weeks earlier. The full moon had sparkled on the water, and the food had been superb. She tried not to recall what it had felt like to be in such an intimate setting with a man like Ross. His hand at her waist, guiding her across the restaurant, had seared her flesh and made her heart race. His fingers had brushed lightly, accidentally across hers, and she'd felt sparks flare up like Fourth of July firecrackers. The sound of his laughter had warmed her, and the look in his eyes had dazzled her.

But it hadn't meant anything, she reminded herself regretfully. The evening had ended, and nothing between them had really changed. Today, having lunch there with this Jason person might be the start of something. And at the very least, it would be the best meal she had all week.

"That will be just fine," she said softly, noting a strange little light in Ross's eyes. It seemed to flicker brightly, then dim at her words. She blinked and shook her head. She must be imagining things.

"See you at noon," she told Jason.

As soon as she'd hung up, Ross gave her a list of

instructions longer than any he'd ever given her to prepare her for a major business meeting. *Go straight into the restaurant. Don't linger in the parking lot. Sit at a table in full view of the other patrons. If the man does anything out of line, excuse yourself and go into the rest room.* Her head was reeling.

"And exactly how long am I supposed to hide out in the rest room?" she demanded.

"Until he leaves."

"What if he waits? Criminals often go to uncommon lengths to wait out their quarry," she observed tartly.

Ross scowled at her sarcasm.

"Just be careful," he muttered as he walked out of the office, the door slamming behind him. Katie stared at the door in surprise, then shrugged. It must have been an accident. Ross Chandler was always in control.

He was also sitting behind a bank of ferns at the seafood restaurant, she discovered when she stopped in the rest room just before asking the maître d' if Jason was there yet. With his face only partially hidden by a newspaper, Ross looked like a furtive private eye. Katie debated killing him on the spot, but finally marched right past him with her head held high. Committing murder on their first date probably would not make a good impression on Jason.

Apparently, though, she didn't quite rid herself of the scowl on her face, because after Jason arrived at their reserved table and they had introduced themselves, the first thing he said was, "Are you okay?"

"Absolutely. I just saw someone I know," she said. "It's nothing."

Jason demonstrated astonishing concern. "Would

you prefer to leave? We could always go somewhere else."

"No. Of course not. Why would I want to leave?"

"You seem to be upset."

Katie gave him one of her most dazzling smiles. "I'm sorry. I'm not upset, just surprised. I hadn't expected to see him again so soon. It's just my boss."

"Oh," Jason said, his tone relieved. Obviously, he had no idea that seeing her boss here, when she'd thought he was having the lunch she'd ordered for him ten miles away in his office, was more disturbing than running into her ex-husband. Seeing Paul Stewart occasionally around town never made her heart flutter the way it was doing now at the knowledge that Ross was just beyond those drooping ferns.

Blast the man, she thought furiously. He hadn't trusted her to be able to handle this on her own. Well, she was going to show him. She was going to have the time of her life. She propped her chin in her hand and gazed intently at Jason. He was tall, dark, and handsome, just as his letter had said.

But not quite as tall as Ross, she noted. Nor did his dark hair have the same ebony sheen as Ross's. And while his appearance was polished, his features even and attractive, they didn't have the strength of character that Ross's did. His build was trim, and as she'd watched him stride through the restaurant to their table, she'd noted his athletic grace; but he didn't vibrate with sexuality the way Ross did.

Good Lord, was she going to start comparing every man she met with her boss? How absurd!

She tried focusing on Jason's obvious strengths. His manner from the moment he'd joined her had been charming, and his sense of humor was just as lively as his note had hinted. He also seemed perceptive and sincere. He did not appear to be a threat.

In fact, she decided midway through her lunch of poached salmon with dill sauce, if she weren't vibrantly—no, disgustingly—aware of Ross sitting just beyond the line of her vision, she would be having a very good time.

Jason told her about his children, and it was obvious that he was devoted to the boys. The breakup of his marriage had been "just one of those things," he said without a trace of bitterness or floundering for excuses.

"It's an old story. We just grew further and further apart. Alex—Alexandra—apparently didn't see it coming, so there were some rough times at first, all sorts of accusations, but there was no truth to them. I wasn't having an affair. I just knew there had to be more to marriage than what we had. I thought we both had a right to try to find it," he said, then smiled. "Your turn. Are you divorced?"

"Yes. I must have been a lot like Alex. I was surprised, too. I mean, how can you live with a man for twelve years, a man you've known since high school, and not realize that everything is falling apart? In our case, there *was* another woman, but the marriage would probably have died from neglect anyway. I can see that now. She just hurried the process along."

"Did he marry her?"

"No. In fact, he started playing the field as though he'd just discovered his adolescence. He'd missed out on it the first time around by falling for me in the tenth grade." Her smile was tinged with sadness. "I hope he finds what he's looking for. He's a good man."

"Are you still in love with him?"

She shook her head, surprised to realize that it was true, that she hadn't been in love with Paul for a long time now. She rarely thought of him, except when he stopped by to pick up Lisa, and then they were able to get along like old friends, rather than like two people who'd shared so much of their lives and had created a vivacious, wonderful child together.

From their personal backgrounds, she and Jason drifted into a discussion of their interests. They had very little in common. He liked sailing; she got seasick. She loved to read, absorbing the information in newspapers and magazines like a sponge and treating each book as an adventure with new friends; he glanced at the sports pages and subscribed to *Sports Illustrated*. He thought Sunday-afternoon football was the greatest thing since the invention of the wheel; she watched concerts on PBS. As they realized how unsuited they were, they laughed.

"Surely there's something we both like," Jason said. "I want to see you again."

"Salmon," Katie noted, holding up a forkful of the flaky fish.

"I'm not sure we can build a relationship around salmon."

Suddenly, the fern quivered, and Katie shot a disbelieving glance in its direction. The next thing she knew, Ross would be climbing over the barrier and sitting down at the table with them. She lowered her voice in a deliberate attempt to elude Ross's prying. It never occurred to her that she was only provoking his interest.

"I'm not sure I want to build a relationship at all," she confessed slowly. "I don't just mean with you. I mean with anyone."

Jason studied her curiously. "Then why the ad?"

She told him the story, and was pleased to see that he seemed to be laughing with her rather than at her. "So your friends set out to turn your dull, boring life around for you?"

"Exactly," she said, noting the brim of a hat poking through the fern. She was tempted to reach over and yank it off. Instead, she kept on talking. "But I don't think my life is dull and boring. I've been having a wonderful time learning to manage on my own. I love my work. I'm really getting to know my daughter. I can order pizza for dinner, if I want to, or go to a Saturday-afternoon movie, instead of cleaning the kitchen."

"I knew it," Jason said gleefully.

"What?"

"Movies. I knew we'd find something, if we talked long enough. We could go to a movie together. There's a great new science-fiction film playing."

Katie winced. "I like foreign films."

He sighed. "I should have known."

"We could still have dinner or something," she suggested bravely. "I mean, I would like to see you again." She was surprised to find that she meant it. She had enjoyed his company, even if there weren't any fireworks exploding inside. Jason was pleasant and comfortable. She'd like to have him as a friend. She'd never had a real male friend before . . . except Ross, and he seemed intent on overstepping the bounds of friendship today.

"As a friend," he said, picking up on her thoughts.

She winced. "Would that be so awful?"

He grinned at her. "Actually, it would be a refreshing change." He took her hand in his as they walked to the door of the restaurant. "I'll call you, Katie Stewart."

"I hope so," she said and watched him walk away, shading her eyes against the glare of the sun.

It was probably the glare of the sun that kept her from seeing Ross until she practically bumped into him. He was pacing up and down beside her car. Katie stopped stock-still and put her hands on her hips. She stared straight up into Ross's eyes—or, rather, his sunglasses. She could see her reflection and she adjusted her expression until it was suitably furious.

"What the hell did you think you were doing following me here?"

"You saw me, huh?"

"Let's just say I wouldn't advise you to apply for undercover work. Now why are you here?"

He took off the sunglasses, and she noted a little glimmer in his eyes that just might have signaled guilt.

"I was worried about you," he admitted.

"You are not my father, Ross Chandler," she said sternly, though she practically had to bite her tongue to keep from chuckling at his thoroughly abashed expression. "Come to think of it, not even my father ever followed me on a date. What were you thinking of?"

"I thought it would be the chivalrous thing to do. You could have gotten in trouble."

"I could have gotten out of it, as well. We were in a public place in broad daylight."

"Okay. You're right. I'm sorry," he said contritely. "How'd it go?"

"It went just fine. From your vantage point be-

hind the fern, did you see any signs of my having to
beat his roving hands away with a fork?"

"No."

"Did you hear him making any particularly lewd
suggestions?"

"No."

"Exactly. He was a perfect gentleman. Very
thoughtful. Considerate. Entertaining."

Ross felt a hard knot forming in his stomach. The
blasted man sounded like a paragon of virtue, and
he'd looked like a damn model. He, on the other
hand, had apparently made a complete jackass of
himself. He'd never seen Katie lose her temper before. If it hadn't been directed quite properly at him,
he might have enjoyed it. He liked a woman with
spirit.

"I suppose you're going to see him again," he said
tightly, fully aware that he'd probably driven her to
doing it just to spite him.

"Yes," she said, opening the door of her car and
slipping inside.

"When?"

She smiled at him brightly. "Soon, I hope," she
said sweetly as she turned on the engine. Ross felt as
though he'd just been punched in the gut. If Katie
didn't watch herself, she could very well develop into
a real go-for-the-jugular businesswoman. She clearly
knew exactly how to hit him where it hurt.

"See you back at the office," she added casually.
"Don't forget you have a two o'clock appointment
and it's already one-fifty."

"Damn!"

"Don't worry," she soothed. "I'll explain that you
got held up at lunch." She taunted him with a wicked

grin that made his heart flip over. "I assume you did get to eat? The salmon was superb."

At $13.95 it probably was, he noted in disgust. His throat had been so dry he hadn't tasted the first bite, and now he didn't even have time to stop for a lousy hamburger.

As Katie pulled away, Ross uttered a string of exceptionally colorful oaths and savagely kicked the tire of his car. If the toe of his Italian leather loafer had been the tiniest bit sharper, the tire probably would have gone flat. It had been that kind of a day.

CHAPTER TWO

Dear Red,
I'm exactly what you're looking for. Call me and let's make beautiful music together.

—Eric

"SOUNDS CONCEITED, if you ask me," Ross muttered over Katie's shoulder the following week. "Are you still getting those damn letters?"

She hadn't even heard Ross walk into her office, but she'd known he was there. An alertness had suddenly come over her, an instinctive awakening of all of her senses. Of course, there'd also been the subtle citrus scent of his after shave, which did the most amazing things to her heartbeat. She must be allergic to the stuff.

"Yes, I'm still getting them, and I didn't ask you," she replied.

He scowled fiercely. "I suppose you're going to call him, too."

She tilted her chin stubbornly. "I just might."

Actually, she'd had no intention of calling Eric. He had sounded a bit arrogant, and he hadn't told her a thing about himself. She might find out more on the phone, but he struck her as being the elusive, superficial sort who would talk a lot but reveal very little about himself under any conditions.

He was probably a taker, not a giver, she decided, then grinned at her instinctive analysis. For a woman who hadn't dated in years, it was amazing what she thought she could pick up from a few lines scrawled hurriedly across a piece of notepaper. The next thing she knew, she'd be taking up handwriting analysis. Eric's note was on yellow legal paper. That said a lot, too. He clearly had not been out to impress her.

Maybe she should call him after all, just to see if she was right. She tried not to think about the effect that call would have on Ross, or whether that thought had anything to do with her change of heart about the cryptic Eric.

"There's no time to call him now," Ross objected, taking up his favorite perch on the corner of her desk, his muscular legs spread-eagled in a most disconcerting pose. Increasingly lately, she'd found her eyes drawn up those legs in a blatantly frank appraisal before blinking and turning away in embarrassment. What the devil was getting into her?

Katie lifted her gaze now and shot Ross a puzzled glance. "Why not? It's Friday night. It's after five. We don't have any more appointments and, in case you've forgotten, we've worked late every night this week."

"I..." He hesitated, then added what to Katie

seemed a hastily contrived excuse. "I want to go over the Simpson proposal with you."

"We went over the Simpson proposal last night and again this morning. We both know every comma and semicolon in it. Why are you so uptight about this deal? You have Roger Simpson exactly where you want him."

"I'm not uptight," he grumbled.

"Then why go over it again?"

"I've had some new thoughts since this morning," he said defensively. "Besides, this is an important deal. We've had several setbacks the last few months, thanks to Dorian Hayes. We have to be prepared. I'll be damned if I'm letting that man get the jump on me again. I don't mind losing out fair and square, but he's an unscrupulous weasel."

"Okay," she relented. "I understand how you feel about Hayes. Exactly how long do you think it will take you to explain these new thoughts? Shall I call Lisa and tell her not to expect me for dinner?" She glanced up at him significantly. "Again."

Ross felt a guilty twinge in the pit of his stomach. He shouldn't keep Katie hanging around the office after hours just to satisfy his . . . his what? His ego? His jealousy? Ever since last week's episode with Jason, he'd felt the stirring of all sorts of strange sensations whenever he was around Katie, but surely they weren't being provoked by jealousy. Concern was more like it. He was worried about her, and that, dammit, was just as troubling.

Katie was his assistant; their relationship was strictly professional. True, they had developed a wonderful rapport over the last ten months, but he had his own, very active social life to lead. In fact, he had a date later tonight with Doreen, a very tall, very sexy, very accommodating stewardess who was flying in from Rio. A woman like Katie Stewart was not his type. She was the hearth-and-home type. She was warm apple pie and Sunday picnics. She was quiet nights, teasing laughter, and commitment. He needed glamour and white-chocolate mousse and tousled satin sheets. He needed freedom. That's why he'd gotten divorced himself.

Or was it? The possibility that Jaclyn had actually initiated the divorce by casting him in the role of guilty party danced through his mind and left him reeling. All those charges she'd leveled at him about being unable to make a commitment must have stuck. Yet, until she'd made them, he'd always thought of himself as a happily married man. Not even his thoughts had strayed.

Still, now that the divorce was a *fait accompli*, he did enjoy dating a wide variety of women. Katie was not the sort to be part of a crowd, and he wasn't ready to risk another encounter with a woman who could shake his self-confidence in the way Jaclyn had. He knew instinctively that Katie could do that, too. He respected her opinions in business. It stood to reason that a personal rejection by her would hurt worse than some turndown by a woman he didn't much care about seeing in the first place.

So, if he wasn't about to ask her on a date himself, what the hell was he doing trying to interfere with her personal time? For a man who exuded self-confidence, Ross felt oddly uncertain. It was not a feeling with which he was comfortable. It was not a feeling he was about to tolerate.

"Forget it," he finally groused. "We can go over the file before the meeting on Monday. Call this Eric person, if you want to." He stalked back into his office and, once again, left Katie staring after him in confusion.

He heard her tidying up her desk, putting papers into her briefcase, and, finally, her musical "good night" as she passed his door. Suddenly, he realized he'd been practically holding his breath, and it wasn't until the outer door closed that he released it with a sigh. She hadn't made that phone call after all. He leaned back in his chair, swiveled around to stare out the window at the darkening sky, and wondered why that made him feel so incredibly good.

Katie felt a momentary pang of loneliness as she rode the elevator down to the ground floor of the building housing Chandler Electronics. She almost regretted not going ahead and calling Eric or one of the other men who'd responded to the ad. It would have been nice to be going out for a drink or dinner now, instead of following the same old routine.

She'd been through all the letters, and she had to admit that several of them were intriguing. The men seemed well-educated, articulate, and, according to what they wrote, simply tired of the bar scene and looking for a new way to meet interesting people. And, as Jennifer had reminded her at the beginning of the week, meeting people was what the ad was all about.

"Maybe Mr. Right won't be in there, but at least you'll make some new friends," she'd encouraged Katie. "What's wrong with that? That Jason guy wasn't so bad, was he?"

"No. He was very nice."

"Has he called?"

"I only met him last Wednesday, Jen. He said he'd call."

"Well, even if he doesn't, there are thirty more."

"Forty."

"Forty?"

"I got ten more today."

"Terrific. If they're not right for you, maybe one of them will have a friend who's just what you're looking for."

"I'm not looking for anyone," Katie had reminded her. "You are."

"Be honest, Katie. Aren't you tired of spending all your time with a ten-year-old?"

"I don't spend all of my time with Lisa. I spend most of it at work." With Ross, she added silently. Intriguing, unavailable Ross, who's been behaving very weirdly lately.

Aloud, she said, "The rest of my time I spend on the phone listening to you and Maggie tell me how to jazz up my life. I think I'll join an aerobics class five nights a week, just to get away from the phone."

Jennifer sighed. "Okay. You've made your point. I won't push."

"Ha!"

"I won't." There had been the longest pause Katie had ever heard in any conversation with her friend. She could practically see Jennifer biting her tongue. Finally, Jennifer had said plaintively, "Couldn't you at least call another one of them?"

Katie's laughter had bubbled forth. "Okay. I'll call. I promise."

But she hadn't called Eric or any of the others. She'd been so busy all week that she'd barely had time to do the grocery shopping and the laundry, and tonight Lisa was having a pajama party, which meant popcorn and pizza and giggling until all hours of the night. She'd spend all day tomorrow just cleaning up the mess, and she'd promised to take Lisa canoeing on Sunday, even though the mere idea of it made her nauseous. Paul had backed out at the last minute, though, and she hated to see Lisa disappointed.

Monday, she vowed. I'll call one of them on Monday.

But on Monday she and Ross were tied up all morning preparing for the meeting with Roger Simpson, who had invented a household robot that Ross wanted to manufacture. According to Simpson and his high-powered attorneys, the miniature robot was supposed to revolutionize homemaking. Katie had her doubts, which she'd already expressed in no uncertain terms. Ross had listened, but she was convinced his mind was made up. He wanted this robot.

When Mr. Mom whirred into the office that afternoon carrying a tray of soft drinks and followed by a very serious entourage of full-grown men in three-piece suits, she almost giggled aloud. Only Ross's cautionary glance stopped her. She greeted the humans, avoided looking Mr. Mom in his blinking green eyes, and sat back in her chair to watch the presentation.

"Today's society is becoming more and more comfortable with the scientific advances that make life easier," Roger Simpson began. "Just look at the number of homes with compact discs, VCRs, and personal computers. We think people are ready to accept a robot like Mr. Mom in their lives. He can cook, clean, serve at parties. He can even be programmed to answer the phone."

An impish vision of leaving Mr. Mom to talk to Jennifer and Maggie flitted through Katie's mind. She almost asked how good the genderless robot was on a date.

"But is he cost-effective?" she asked instead, ignoring Ross's subtle signals not to be negative. She couldn't have kept her mouth shut another minute if he'd threatened to fire her on the spot. She might not have years of business experience, but she'd been a homemaker for long enough to know the demands of that job. Nothing would ever convince her a robot was up to them.

"If you consider what you'd have to pay a maid to do all of these things over an extended period of time, absolutely," Mr. Simpson said confidently.

"But most people don't have maids," Katie countered. "And I haven't needed a replacement part in years. Can Mr. Mom claim that?"

Roger Simpson paled and glanced at Mr. Mom almost as if he expected the robot to be embarrassed. Mr. Mom's green eyes were staring solemnly straight ahead. Apparently, his repertoire did not include blushing at an intimate discussion of his parts.

"Actually, we think a five-year warranty period would be quite adequate. Manufactured and programmed properly, in fact, there's no reason for anything to go wrong for at least that long, possibly longer."

"Sounds like the perfect mate for a confirmed bachelor," she muttered under her breath, casting a significant glance in Ross's direction. "No muss. No fuss. And only a five-year commitment."

"Would you like to see a few of the things Mr. Mom can do?"

"Absolutely," Ross said, so enthusiastically that Katie knew she'd been right: He was going to buy this patent no matter how ridiculous she thought it to be. His reaction was typical of a grown man who didn't have enough toys to play with. Last year it had been a child-size motorized car for the eight-year-old who was tried of walking. Katie's moans of dismay over that one had been ignored as well. To be truthful, Ross had been right. Apparently, there were more wealthy, indulgent parents than she'd realized.

"Mr. Mom responds to over a hundred basic voice commands and can be programmed for many more, depending on the needs of the individual buyer," Simpson explained proudly. "Why don't you ask him to do something?" he suggested to Ross.

Ross looked exactly like a teenager given the chance to drive an outrageously expensive foreign sports car. "Answer the phone," he commanded Mr. Mom.

The robot swiveled around until he sighted the phone, then whirred across the room and picked up the receiver. "Hello," he said in a monotone. "No one is home now. You may leave a message at the sound of the tone." A high-pitched beep followed.

"Any old answering machine can do that," Katie protested. "I want to see Mr. Mom cook dinner, wash the dishes, iron the clothes, and get the kids to bed."

Mr. Mom's eyes blinked frantically, and he whirled around in a circle, his metal arms flailing. A frantic grinding that might have been interpreted as a frustrated groan came from deep inside him. Katie's eyes widened, and even Ross seemed stunned.

"What's wrong with him?" she asked.

"Stop, Mr. Mom. It's okay," Simpson said, immediately soothing the robot to a standstill. He and Mr. Mom scowled at Katie until she felt thoroughly chastised. "You gave him four commands at once, and all for things he couldn't possibly do in here. He was looking for the kitchen, the ironing board, and the kids."

"Sorry," she mumbled, then realized she was apologizing not to Roger Simpson, but to an absurdly expensive hunk of metal. She was clearly losing it. Ross caught her eye, and this time he winked. Suddenly, the warmth of sunshine filled her, and she found herself smiling back at him as if the two of them were sharing a wonderful secret.

"I'm going to have to think about this a little longer," Ross said. Roger Simpson's face fell, and his attorneys looked stunned. They'd walked in here this afternoon expecting to close a deal. It was probably all her fault that they hadn't, Katie thought.

As soon as they'd left, she looked contritely at Ross and said, "I'm sorry. I blew it, didn't I? I know I'm not supposed to play devil's advocate at these meetings, but I couldn't stand it. That . . . that thing, posing as some sort of mechanized, twenty-first century housewife, made me crazy."

Ross grinned at her, picked her up, and twirled her around until she was giddy. Suddenly, Katie wasn't aware of anything except the hard strength of Ross's arms around her waist and the warmth of his body pressed against hers. Nerves that had lain dormant since the divorce—no, even longer that that—crackled to life and sent sparks ricocheting through her.

"You were wonderful," he said, kissing her soundly on the cheek. Another fire sparked, then burst into flame. "Absolutely wonderful!"

"I was?" she asked dazedly.

"Of course," he said. "Now I'll be able to get that patent for a song. After listening to you, Simpson's bound to be convinced I'm not going to want it at all. By tomorrow he'll be ready to bargain."

Katie slid slowly down the length of Ross's body

until her feet touched the floor. As his hands fell away, her own hands went to her hips. "You mean you're actually going to buy that thing? I thought you'd changed your mind, once you saw how silly it was."

"Of course I'm going to buy it. It'll do great at Christmas. I can just see it featured in all of the classiest catalogs as the perfect gift for your friends who have everything."

"You're crazy. If people have enough money for Mr. Mom, they have enough money for a maid or a housekeeper. They don't want some mechanical nitwit who gets confused if you tell him to do more than one thing at a time."

"We can work that out. We'll program him to accept lists of chores in priority order."

"Heaven forbid that he gets a glitch in his system and puts the kids in the dishwater."

Ross scowled at her lack of enthusiasm. "It wouldn't kill them."

"Maybe not, but have you ever tried to fit a ten-year-old in the kitchen sink?"

Katie couldn't help it. Suddenly, she was giggling and then Ross was laughing and then she was in his arms and they were spinning around again until they were both so dizzy they could hardly stand. At least that's what she told herself, when she found that she was clinging to Ross, her hands locked behind his neck, her fingers buried in the ebony silk of his hair.

She was caught up in a wild sensation of recklessness, of utter abandon, fueled by the raging heat of their bodies and the sheer excitement and unfettered joy of the moment. She hadn't felt this way in years. No, she corrected, she had never felt quite this way before, as if the days were filled with endless possibilities and the nights could be sparked by magic.

Ross's eyes met hers, and immediately the laughter died, chased away by far more serious emotions, puzzling emotions that had nothing to do with robots or business meetings or the casual banter that made up their usual days.

"I . . . I have to go," Katie said softly, pulling away, retreating behind a wall of polite office decorum. Ross, who seemed equally shaken, stayed on the other side of that wall.

"You have plans?"

She nodded.

"One of those men?"

She nodded again.

"I see," he said, his tone flat. "Thanks for your help this afternoon."

She smiled shakily. "No problem. It's what you pay me to do."

"So . . ."

Katie waited until finally he backed through the door. "See you in the morning," he said, giving her a jaunty salute.

"Good night, Ross."

After he had left, she realized her hands were clenched so tightly that her knuckles had turned white. Why had she lied to him? Why had she told him she had a date tonight, when the only things on her agenda were washing her hair and helping Lisa with an English essay?

Because, you ninny, with very little encouragement, you could fall for Ross Chandler, and that would be like Cinderella expecting to wind up with Prince Charming.

Her lips curved into a soft smile. But that's exactly

what *had* happened, she reminded herself, then brought herself up short. She might be attractive and bright, but she was no match for those glamorous beauties who flitted in and out of Ross's life like bees in search of nectar to make honey.

Besides, she had forty men who *were* interested in her, or at least in meeting her. Why waste her time daydreaming about a man who wasn't the least bit interested in a relationship that lasted longer than the morning after?

Decisively, she pulled out the letter from Eric and dialed his number. She'd consider tonight an experiment, sort of a test of her dating skills. She might as well practice with someone she knew instinctively was not her type at all. If Eric was as arrogant as he seemed, all she'd need to do would be nod occasionally.

Two hours later, she was drinking her third club soda and lime and trying very hard not to die of boredom. Only the nodding was keeping her awake.

Eric, it turned out, not only had the conceit of a matinee idol without the looks, he had the mentality of a model train with a single track. He was a salesman whose only goal was the selling of Eric. Katie had wanted to leave after the first drink, but politeness had kept her perched on a barstool, twirling a swizzle stick around in her glass and wondering where on earth Eric had found a jacket in that exact combination of mismatched colors.

"You know, honey, you have the greatest eyes," he said, drawing her attention away from the jarring green, red, and brown plaid.

"Thank you."

"I'd like to see those eyes when you're all sleepy and passionate."

Katie gulped. "I beg your pardon."

"Come on, honey. You and I could really have something together. Don't you feel it?"

What she felt was sick to her stomach, Katie thought, but managed to refrain from saying it. "No. No, I don't believe so," she said with her least encouraging smile. "And I really must be going."

"You can't leave now," Eric protested. "We're just getting to know each other."

"I have to get home to my daughter. I don't like to leave her alone too late."

"It's only eight o'clock."

"Well, you know how kids are. Once it's dark, they can get into all sorts of mischief." She slid off the barstool and held out her hand. "Thank you so much for the drinks, Eric."

"No problem, honey. I'll give you a call real soon and we'll do it again."

Over my dead body, Katie thought, but said only, "That would be lovely." She figured it was a safe enough comment, as long as Eric didn't realize until after she'd left that she'd never mentioned her last name, her address, her phone number, or any other identifying trace. Unless he was a detective with the skills of Mike Hammer, she would never see him again. For all of his smooth flattery, she doubted if he thought she was worth the effort.

At home, she found the stereo blaring, the television on, and Lisa lying on the floor with her feet propped on the wall, talking on the phone. She'd never seen a more welcome sight in her life.

By the time she'd turned off everything that was making noise—with the exception of Lisa—and made herself a snack of cheese and crackers, her daughter was off the phone.

"Hi, Mom. How was the big date?"

"Awful."

"You missed some calls."

"I'm amazed you were off the phone long enough for any calls to come in."

"Cute."

"Who called?"

"Jennifer. I told her you were out with one of those guys."

"Did she want me to call back?"

"No. She said to tell you to go for it."

Katie grimaced. "Anybody else call?"

"Some guy named Ross. Isn't that your boss's name?"

Ross had called here? He never called her at home. "Did he say what he wanted?" She hoped she sounded only casually interested.

"Nope, but it must have been important."

"Why?"

"Because he's been calling every half hour. He should be checking in again in the next couple of minutes."

Katie got the oddest sensation in the pit of her stomach, and the memory of Ross's arms tight around her made her pulse skitter crazily. She took her plate into the kitchen, told Lisa to finish her homework, and started up the stairs.

"Oh," she said casually. "If Ross calls again, tell him I've called in and you don't expect me for hours."

Lisa blinked at her, then grinned. "Hey, all right, Mom," she said. "I think you're catching on."

Katie chuckled in spite of herself. "And I think

you're beginning to remind me of Jennifer and Maggie," she retorted, then raced up the stairs just as the phone started ringing. By the time she reached the top step, she was already feeling guilty. What if it was something important? It must be for Ross to be making repeated calls to the house. She turned to go back just in time to see Lisa put the receiver back in the cradle.

"Well?" she said.

"It was Ross. I told him what you said."

"And?"

"He sounded kind of funny, but he said to tell you he'd see you in the morning."

Katie stood indecisively in the middle of the staircase, pondering the message. If the calls hadn't been about business, what had they been about? Was it possible that Ross had been checking up on her again? If so, why?

As if she'd been reading her mind, Lisa giggled and offered one possibility. "I think the guy's got the hots for you, Mom."

"Lisa!"

"Well, I do. And if he looks anything like he sounds, I'd go for it."

"Ross Chandler is my boss. That's all."

"Right," Lisa said skeptically.

Katie scowled at her daughter. "Don't you have homework to do?"

"I've finished."

"Then go to bed."

"It's barely nine o'clock."

"Well, do something," Katie muttered in frustration. She wanted to go upstairs, soak in a hot bubble bath, and try to figure out if there was any possibility that Lisa might be right. As ten-year-olds went, the kid was very bright. It would be disconcerting as hell to discover that she was also uncommonly perceptive.

CHAPTER THREE

Dear Redhead,

I've never done this before, but your ad struck a responsive chord in me. I'm recently divorced and not used to this dating business yet. I'm not comfortable in bars, and my best friends are married and absolutely refuse to let me date their wives. I guess we're just an old-fashioned bunch. What about you? Are you old-fashioned? You say you have varied interests. What have you read lately? Do you like Beethoven? Can you put up with a workaholic who still finds time to be nice to his mother? If so, give me a call. You sound friendly and everyone can use a friend.

Yours, Ken

ROSS COULDN'T HELP it. The letter was lying right there on top of Katie's desk, out where anyone could see it. He skimmed it, then threw it down, aware that a part of him was hoping the damn thing would slide into the trash can and be buried under a ton of wadded-up scrap paper. He dumped several file folders on top of it, instead. Maybe she wouldn't find it again for a month.

He wondered if she'd called this one yet. Or was this the guy she'd gone out with last night? The one who'd kept her out until all hours? The thought of Katie out having the time of her life with some pervert who'd take advantage of her innocence had kept him awake half the night.

He'd spent the other half of the night trying to figure out why he was worrying. As Katie had reminded him several times lately, she was a grown woman, capable of making her own decisions and fending off her own suitors. She was not his responsibility. Nor did he have any claims on her.

Yet a part of him felt that her professional flowering under his tutelage these last months gave him both responsibilities and rights where she was concerned. He'd watched an insecure housewife blossom into a self-confident businesswoman. He ought to be thrilled to pieces that she was now ready to rediscover her value as a woman as well.

He hated it.

"Ross?" There was an edge of surprise in Katie's voice as she walked back into her office and saw him standing beside her desk, a frown on his face. "Did you need something?"

"Nope," he said, smiling at her. The smile seemed forced, but it did the most amazing things to her insides anyway, especially after the startlingly sensual images she'd spent the night conjuring up. "I just stopped in to see how the big date went."

While her back was to him, Katie made a wry grimace, then turned and sank down in her chair. Avoiding the question, she said, "I heard you'd called."

"Several times."

"Any particular reason? Was there a problem with the Simpson project?"

Suddenly, Ross, whose every move was normally decisive, looked exceedingly flustered. "No. No problem. Not exactly, anyway. I just needed to talk to you."

Katie waited. Ross paced. He was clearly unnerved, and though she couldn't be sure why, she loved it. Trying not to grin, Katie silently watched and waited some more.

"Oh, hell," he finally said, glaring at her. "I was worried about you. I don't like all these weird dates you're having."

"I thought we'd already had this discussion. What's weird about these dates? You probably meet women in bars all the time and ask them out. You don't know them any better than I know these men."

"That's different."

"Why?"

"Because I can take care of myself."

Katie chuckled. "I wasn't worried about *you*. I was thinking of the women."

"Right. Of course." He flushed with embarrassment and paced some more. His agitation and frustration were worse than a caged lion's. "I still don't like it."

Katie sighed and admitted honestly, "To tell you the truth, I'm not all that comfortable with it either, but Jennifer and Maggie were right about one thing: It is time I started meeting men again and going out. This is one way to do it."

"Isn't there a better way?"

"If there is, I haven't run across it. You men have it easy. If you see a woman you like, you just walk up and introduce yourself. On top of that, you're on every guest list as the extra man. No one ever seems to need an extra woman."

"That can't be true. Surely one of your friends can introduce you to someone."

"My friends are the ones who wrote the ad," she reminded him.

"Then join a group or something."

"I have a full-time job and a full-time daughter. I don't have time for groups. I'm trying the 'or something.'"

He gazed at her curiously. "Do you want to get married again?" There was an odd tentativeness to the question.

"How did we jump from dating to marriage?"

"It's a logical progression."

"Not for you," she pointed out.

"We aren't talking about me. What about you?"

"No," she said honestly and without a moment's hesitation. From the moment Paul had left, it was the one thing she'd felt certain about. She'd made one mistake, choosing a man who would keep her tied to hearth and home; she wasn't about to make another. More and more lately, she'd wanted to rediscover the old Katie, the one who'd taken any dare, the one who'd dreamed of traveling and excitement and silk nightgowns trimmed in French lace before more practical notions had settled in. No, she wasn't looking for marriage.

"But I would like some adult companionship," she said. "After a while, it gets tiresome always being the third wheel with your married friends."

Ross's eyes widened to fathomless dark pools of disbelief. "You mean you want to have an affair?" His voice fairly quivered with astonishment.

Her lips twitched, and she barely restrained her laughter. She was no more ready to have an affair than she was to leap from the Space Needle, but she couldn't resist teasing Ross. "You seem shocked," she said innocently. "Isn't that what liberated women do in the eighties? Isn't that what you do?"

"We're talking about you, not me," he grumbled, a frown on his lips. His eyes turned stormy. "You're different, Katie. You can't just go around having flings."

"Why not?"

"Because . . ."

"Because why?" she persisted.

"Because it's just not right, dammit!"

"Because it doesn't fit your image of me? What *is* your image of me, Ross?" Katie was genuinely curious. He obviously didn't view her as a sex object, more's the pity. Hell, she didn't see herself as a sex object. In her case, it had something to do with those flannel nightgowns, no doubt. But Ross had never seen her in a nightgown, flannel or otherwise. If anyone knew the Katie she was trying to become again, it was Ross. He'd watched her evolution. He'd encouraged it, in fact.

"You're intelligent, sensitive, cheerful. You're a terrific mother. You probably even bake apple pies." There was a strangely wistful note in his voice, but Katie was too busy being insulted to pay much attention to it.

Lordy, she sounded dull. It also stunned her to realize that, despite the changes she saw in herself, and had assumed he saw, too, Ross thought of her as the old Katie. She shook her head. At least he recognized her intelligence. That ought to count for something.

"I hate to let you down, but I do not bake apple pies," she stated finally. "I don't even bake chocolate-chip cookies. Any baking that gets done in our house, Lisa does. In fact, she's probably better at fixing dinner than I am. I'd be content with frozen dinners and an occasional backyard barbecue, if I didn't feel a sense of duty to give Lisa proper vegetables and broiled chicken occasionally."

Ross's expression couldn't have been more astounded if she'd casually dismissed both Santa Claus and the tooth fairy in the presence of an impressionable three-year-old. He had apparently built up one hell of an idealized image of her.

"If you didn't cook, what did you do all those years you spent at home?" He seemed honestly puzzled.

"In case you're not aware of it, the vast majority of food requires very little time to prepare, especially if you own a microwave oven," she said, giving him a wry grin and wondering if his attitude had anything to do with his divorce. He seemed to be living in another era. "Spending all day whipping out some gourmet fare that would be eaten in twenty minutes was not my idea of heaven. I spent as little time on cooking as possible. I did all of those other ordinary, housewifely tasks, too. I took the clothes to the cleaners, dusted under the beds at least once a month, tore down the wallpaper, put up the wallpaper, took Lisa to the park and play school, and knitted. I have an entire drawer filled with sweaters with uneven sleeves and dropped stitches. I even joined groups back then."

As he listened to the litany, Ross felt as though the world were finally righting itself on its axis. This was exactly how he thought of Katie, doing little chores around the house, sitting in front of a fire with colorful yarn, making a pleasant, comfortable home for her husband and daughter. He was so busy reconstructing his perfect image of her, he missed the odd little edge to her voice. Her next comment hit him like a blow below the belt.

"I was miserable," she said with such heartfelt sincerity that he couldn't doubt her. He simply stared at her as if she'd uttered a blasphemy.

"You were?" he said, his voice barely above a whisper. He felt completely baffled. He felt betrayed. It reassured him a little that Katie seemed equally startled by the admission.

"Do you know, I've never said that before to anyone," she marveled. "I'm not even sure I realized it until just now. I did all the right things. I was a good mother, a good wife . . ." She stared at Ross, her blue eyes wide with surprise. ". . . and an incomplete woman."

"You really were miserable?" he repeated, as though she might change her mind if given time to think about what she'd said.

"Yes," she said slowly. "I think I was. Oh, in the beginning I was very much in love and I thought it was all terribly romantic, but as time went on I think I began to want exactly the kind of life I have now. I love having my mind engaged in something more challenging than making up a shopping list. Paul never gave me credit for even having a mind. Our liveliest conversations were over the price of beef and whether we could afford it. We never talked about books or music or politics. He never discussed his business decisions with me the way you do."

"Why on earth not?"

"Probably because we married so young that he couldn't possibly view me in any other way than as his wife. That was all I'd ever been, except a student. Now that I think about it, if I'd spent another ten years in that marriage, my brain probably would have atrophied."

Ross couldn't even begin to imagine such a waste. Paul Stewart must have been blind if he hadn't realized what a sharp, intuitive woman he had in Katie. Then, again, maybe he owed Paul one for leaving her a mental virgin, just waiting for him to lead her into her intellectual womanhood. And, yet, was he one bit better? He liked the thought of Katie at home in the kitchen just as much as Paul apparently had. It had always made him feel good to think there were women like that left in the world. Talk about contradictory feelings!

"I doubt if you'd let that happen," he told her now. "Sooner or later, you'd have found an outlet. In fact, that's probably why you were so active in the PTA. It gave you a chance to test yourself as a leader. A lot of great businesswomen got their starts doing volunteer work."

"Why, Ross Chandler, are you saying that I'm a great businesswoman?" Her infectious grin taunted him; those blue eyes danced with laughter, and instinctively he sensed a carefully set trap.

"You're very good," he hedged, his eyes narrowing. "Why?"

"I was just wondering if this was the right time to ask for a raise."

"My God, I've created a monster. I just gave you a raise last month," he protested.

She sighed. "So you did. Oh, well, it was worth a shot with all that praise being tossed about."

He pointed to *The Wall Street Journal* and the stack of file folders he'd placed on her desk. "Read those and see if you can figure out why Dorian Hayes is always one step ahead of us in the marketplace these days. I know we have better engineers, but we can't seem to get the jump on Hayes. The guy's up to something."

"Aren't you just a little paranoid about this?"

"I know Hayes. We went to school together. He's capable of doing just about anything, including setting out to ruin me."

"But why?"

"Let's just say we had our differences over ethics back then. I won. He lost. He's still trying to get even."

Katie's eyes blinked wide. "How serious is it?"

"It's happened enough to worry me."

Her lips curved into a frown. "Could you lose the company?"

"I hope we can get to the bottom of it before it comes to that."

"Is that why you want that stupid robot so much?"

"Partly." He grinned suddenly. "I also think Mr. Mom is sort of sexy."

"Humph! If that's your idea of sexy, all those women of yours are going to be horribly disappointed."

Ross grimaced at her casual reference to his women. Little did she know how much those glossy, sophisticated beauties bored him after a few dates. They had no substance, no warmth.

"Just read the files," he said gruffly. "If you find something I missed, you'll get your raise."

She beamed at him and his pulse danced more erotically than the tango. "Terrific. I love a challenge."

What Ross loved was the possibility that this distraction might prevent her from calling another one of those men. In fact, if he tried very hard, maybe he could keep her so busy those men would all have married or moved away by the time she got around to calling.

Katie spent the afternoon reading through the material Ross had left, jotting down notes, turning every now and then to stare out the window and try to absorb and interpret what she'd read. What she'd told Ross was absolutely true. She loved a challenge, and it thrilled her that Ross trusted her to take on a project like this. She knew how much Chandler Electronics meant to him. If there was any threat to his hanging on to the company, she was determined to find it.

It was only when she picked up the last folder that she found the letter from Ken. She'd forgotten all about it, but suddenly she felt like taking a break and, before she could stop to think about it, she dialed his number.

This time, when a secretary answered, she felt far more confident than she had when she'd made that first call to Jason. She explained immediately that she was calling on a personal matter and was put right through. She was beginning to feel like an old hand at this by now, though there were a few little butterflies in her stomach when Ken actually got on the line.

"Umm, hi," she said softly. "This is Katie Stewart. You don't know me, but you answered my ad."

"Let me guess," he said lightly. "'Feisty, independent redhead.'"

"That's amazing. You could tell that from my voice?"

"Nope," he admitted sorrowfully. "It's the only ad I've answered. I'm glad you called. You're restoring my confidence."

"Was it shattered?"

"Into little pieces. Your call came just in the nick of time. My secretary was about to call in repairmen, and you know how horribly expensive that can be. I'd probably have been forced into bankruptcy. My children would starve."

Katie was chuckling. "What about your ex-wife?"

"I don't mind if she starves," he said with feigned haughtiness.

"That's not very nice."

"Did I say I was a nice man?"

"Come to think of it, no, but you are. I can tell."

"Ahh," he sighed appreciatively. "Another piece of my confidence just fell into place."

"You're a little crazy."

"Life is crazy. Why don't we meet, and I can explain it to you. I'd hate to think that you're missing out on any of the important stuff."

Katie's head was beginning to reel. Ken was zany, exactly the way she had once been, only now such craziness seemed to throw her. "The important stuff?" she repeated cautiously.

"You know, like skydiving, hang-gliding, hot-air ballooning."

"Do you have something against being on the ground?"

"Of course not, but being up in the air gives you a whole new perspective. You'll see."

"I will?"

"Why don't we do something on Saturday?"

Katie took a deep breath. She'd always wanted to expand her horizons . . . a little, anyway. The most adventurous thing Paul had ever risked was doing the crossword puzzle in ink. "Sure," she said finally.

"Which would you like to do?"

If she had to get off the ground, what she really wanted to do was fly over Mount Rainier and take pictures. She'd been wanting to practice her photography, and what better subject could she have than the spectacular mountain with its snowcapped peak? She suggested it.

"Not very daring," Ken chided her.

"I'm not sure I'm ready to be any more daring than that. I'm out of practice."

"Well, if you insist, then that's what we'll do. As long as we're going up in a plane, I don't suppose you'd like to try skydiving?" he suggested hopefully.

"Not on your life, but if you want to take a plunge, be my guest. I'll take pictures."

"No," he said with what sounded like a tiny sigh of relief. "I'll stick with you."

"I'm a little confused about something," Katie said.

"What's that?"

"Your letter said you were old-fashioned. You don't sound the least bit old-fashioned."

"I'm trying to change."

"You mean you don't regularly do all of those things you talked about?"

"Actually, I've never done any of them," he confessed. "My ex-wife said I was boring."

"Don't you think taking up skydiving might be overreacting just a bit? I mean, it can be dangerous."

"She didn't think so. She did it all the time."

"I see," Katie said thoughtfully. "Ken, tell the truth. How long have you been divorced?"

"A month."

"Whose idea was it?"

"My wife's. Why?"

"It shows."

"Oh, dear. I've blown it, haven't I?"

"You haven't blown it. We've never even met. I just think you might want to wait a little longer before you start a wild orgy of dating."

"Oh, my God," he moaned. "Is that what I've just blown? A wild orgy?"

Katie felt herself blushing. "No. I didn't mean that at all. I'm not . . . I mean I don't . . . Let's just say on that score I'm pretty old-fashioned, too."

"Are you sure you want to break our date for Saturday?"

"I think so. Why don't you call your ex-wife? As long as you're going to be taking up all these crazy activities to prove something to her, you might as well invite her along to watch."

"Now why didn't I think of that?"

"Because you have no self-confidence."

"*Had* no self-confidence," he reminded her. "Remember, you fixed it."

She grinned. "So you said."

"Thanks, Katie. I was right about you."

"Oh?"

"You *are* a friend."

"That's the nicest thing anyone's said to me lately."

"Let's stay in touch."

"I'd like that," she said, and this time she did give out her phone number. "I expect a full report on the skydiving."

"Right. I'll call you next week."

"Bye, Ken," she said, and hung up the phone with a pleased expression.

Skydiving? Ken? Ross thought as he stood in the doorway and waited for Katie to finish her conversation.

"Forget it," he exploded, a grim expression settling on his face and his eyes practically begging for a challenge.

"Forget what?"

"Skydiving. It's too dangerous. You're not going."

Katie glanced up and gave him an unexpected, dazzling smile. "No," she said softly, "I'm not."

"Oh."

Then her expression changed, and he could see the little glint of steel in her eyes, which he'd learned to recognize as a warning signal. It seemed to be appearing more frequently lately.

"But if I were going, Ross Chandler," she said with menace in her voice, "don't you think for one minute that you could stop me."

As she flounced out of the office, Ross realized too late that he had just jammed his size-ten foot smack in the middle of his mouth again.

CHAPTER FOUR

Hi!

*My name is Warren. I'm 37 years old, 6'1",
and weigh about 180 as long as I don't skip
going to the gym. I'm an accountant. I like the
outdoors, camping, water sports, and that sort
of thing. I would also like to get married, but I
guess I just haven't met the right person yet.
Could you be that person? Hope you'll call, so
we can find out.*

"I LIKE THIS one," Jennifer said, as she sat in the
middle of Katie's living room floor sorting through
the stack of responses to the ad. "He sounds sincere."

Katie took the letter Jennifer held out, read it,
and shook her head. "No way."

"Why not?"

"He wants to get married."

"So what? You don't think he'll expect to do it on the first date, do you?"

Katie scowled at her. "I suppose not."

"Then call him. He likes the outdoors. You like the outdoors. That's certainly better than some of these," she said, gesturing toward a stack of rejects, including two Xeroxed form letters that had simply had her box number written in.

"Jennifer, this isn't working," Katie protested with a little sigh. "The guy I called yesterday was still clearly in love with his ex-wife. The one before that was in love with himself. Jason and I didn't have anything in common."

"But that's still three men you didn't know a couple of weeks ago. Remember the cliché . . ." Jennifer paused and bit her lip thoughtfully. "Or maybe it was a greeting card. Anyway, it says you have to kiss a lot of frogs before you find a prince."

"Meaning?"

"That you can't give up after two dates and one phone call. There may be a prince in here."

"And you think this Warren is the one?"

"Maybe. Maybe not, but I think he has definite possibilities."

"Give me the letter," Katie said with a sigh. She might as well get it over with. Jennifer was not likely to leave until she'd made at least one phone call. Hopefully, she wouldn't hold out for an engagement.

After talking to Warren for nearly an hour, with Jennifer blatantly eavesdropping and nodding enthusiastically at Katie's end of the conversation, they made a date for the weekend to go canoeing. It was not what she would have chosen for a first date. A sea-green complexion didn't do her any favors.

Warren had been adamant, though. He seemed to

have an unyielding stubborn streak that did not bode well for the future of the relationship. Katie would have backed out entirely, but with Jennifer waiting hopefully, she didn't dare. Jennifer would only have insisted that she make another call. Besides, how awful could one date be? Maybe he was just having a bad night.

"I expect you to call me the minute you get home on Saturday," Jennifer said as she left. "I just have this feeling this date will be the start of something."

Katie groaned. "If you ever get divorced, Jennifer Gleason, you'd better leave town, because I intend to remind you of every minute of this torture you're putting me through," she said.

A master at inspiring guilt, Jennifer frowned, managing to look hurt at the same time.

"It's not supposed to be torture," she said stiffly. Predictably enough, Katie immediately felt guilt nibbling at her. "You're supposed to have fun. Relax, Katie. Let yourself go. Stop analyzing everything and enjoy yourself. It's only for the day, after all. It's not a commitment."

"I'll try," Katie promised. After all, she'd survived her canoeing expedition with Lisa.

Saturday, however, did not exactly start out in the laugh-a-minute category Jennifer'd had in mind. The morning dawned through a typical autumn fog, layers of gray mist that shadowed Seattle's natural beauty and left it cold and damp. The fog was just beginning to lift by eleven, when Warren was due. By eleven-thirty, when pale fingers of sunlight were dappling the lawn, Katie was muttering about inconsiderate men and pacing around the house with Lisa trailing after her.

"Mom, the guy's only a little late."

"He could have called. Remember that, Lisa. There is never a good excuse for rudeness. Don't ever let yourself be taken advantage of by some thoughtless man—or woman, for that matter. If you let someone get away with it the first time, it establishes a pattern. Stand up for yourself."

"Right, Mom," Lisa soothed. "Why don't you sit down and have another cup of coffee? I'll get it."

"If I have any more coffee, I'll only have to go to the rest room the minute we get to the park."

"Are you nervous or something?"

"No. Why would you ask something like that?"

"Because you're biting your nails. You don't have to go out with this guy, you know. I won't squeal on you, if you cancel."

"I know that. I *want* to go."

"Right." Lisa rolled her eyes.

When the doorbell finally rang, she raced Katie to get it. Katie shooed her away.

"You afraid the guy won't like kids?"

Katie shot her a perplexed look. "What on earth . . . Of course not."

"Then why can't I stay?"

"Because this is bad enough without you standing here looking over my shoulder. It reminds me of when I was in high school and your father used to come over and my father would sit in his easy chair and scowl at the two of us over the top of his newspaper."

"Sounds grim," Lisa agreed. "Okay, I'll go. Have a good one, Mom," she added as she bounded up the stairs.

Katie glanced at her watch as she opened the door. Warren was forty-five minutes late. Instead of apologizing, he came in complaining about her directions. Since she prided herself on being precise with such things, shunning the image of a flighty female who couldn't even get the simplest route to her own house right, she found herself immediately on the defensive. By the time they drove across town to Green Lake, Warren's mood had settled into something slightly more reasonable, but Katie's was rapidly deteriorating. Her instincts about his uncompromising demeanor on the phone were being borne out. It promised to be a very long day.

Then, to top it off, just as they were putting Warren's canoe in the water, Ross magically appeared carrying a strangely familiar-looking canoe. Since he had never once in the last ten months mentioned that he enjoyed canoeing, it couldn't have been a coincidence, though how the devil he'd found out about this date was beyond her. As for the canoe, well, she was probably mistaken. All canoes looked pretty much alike.

At the sight of Ross, dark and masculine and sexy in his shorts and form-fitting knit shirt, Katie's heart leaped into her throat, her pulse raced, and her blood heated up by several degrees. Then she recovered from his assault on her senses and vowed to kill him.

"Excuse me," she muttered to Warren, and stalked over to where Ross was struggling with what she was now convinced was a canoe he'd never before laid eyes on. He seemed to have no idea how to handle it. She stood there with her hands on her own khaki-clad hips, until he finally looked up at her from his bent-over position. He straightened and tried for a surprised expression, but failed miserably. She'd seen pictures of convicted killers looking less guilty.

"What are you doing here?" she hissed furiously.

Ross gazed at her tolerantly, amusement glimmering in his eyes. "Isn't that obvious?" he said, gesturing toward the canoe. "What about you?"

"What's obvious is that you followed me again."

"Why would I do that?"

"Why, indeed? I just want you to know that I don't like it. On Monday morning, we are going to have a little talk about your interference in my life."

"We could talk now," he suggested, a hopeful gleam replacing the amusement in his eyes. "We could go for a walk. The air's crisp. The sun's just coming out. The leaves are turning all these gorgeous fall colors. I even think I hear some music from the other side of the lake. A walk would be great."

"I came here to go canoeing. I am going canoeing." She wondered exactly what kind of a masochist would insist on getting in a canoe with a man she didn't much like when a man she found heart-stoppingly attractive had just given her an alternative.

"Care to go canoeing with me, then?" Ross said, offering yet another option that she refused to take. Sick. She was definitely sick.

"I have a date, thank you."

Ross shrugged. "Whatever you say." He glanced across at Warren. "The guy looks mad." His voice softened. "Be careful, Katie."

"Monday," she huffed, and stomped back to join Warren, who had been watching the exchange with interest. He did, indeed, look mad. In fact, his expression was fierce, reflecting a jealousy he had no right to feel. What had she gotten herself into? She could have had a nice, pleasant afternoon sitting in some movie, a French farce maybe, laughing her head off and munching on a huge tub of buttered

popcorn. Instead, here she was playing tug-of-war
with two ridiculously possessive men who seemed to
think of her as the rope.

"Who the hell was that?" Warren grumbled. "You
have some bodyguard trailing you around?"

"Something like that," Katie said, torn between
fury at Warren's overbearing attitude and her desire
to rip the sexy black hairs off Ross's handsome head
one by one.

"I'm not much on competition. Like I said in my
note, I want to get married. If that guy's got first
claim on you, I'll bow out now. I haven't got time to
waste on a lost cause."

"Charming," Katie muttered under her breath.
Aloud, she insisted, "He has no claim whatsoever on
me."

Despite her statement that Ross meant nothing to
her, she couldn't seem to keep her gaze from straying
over to catch a quick glimpse of him as he paddled
awkwardly around the lake, the muted sunlight glistening on his hair, the muscles in his arms tightening
impressively as he pulled his paddle through the
water.

For all of his protests that he'd merely come out
for a Saturday-afternoon diversion, he remained
within view of Katie at all times. She had a feeling
that if she'd gone to the rest room, he'd have stood
watch outside the door. In some perverse way, she
realized she was beginning to get just the tiniest
sense of satisfaction from his protectiveness. When
she got past her fury, she felt warm inside.

If only she understood why he was doing it. Then
again, maybe she understood only too well. Ross was
a kind man. He wouldn't want to stand by and watch
her get hurt. Unfortunately, he was getting too close,

sneaking past her defenses. She was beginning to feel something more, and she knew it would be a dreadful mistake to let him assume too large a role in her life. It was one thing to daydream about the man occasionally, but it was another entirely to start having false expectations just because he seemed to have developed an untimely and unexpected big-brother complex. Protectiveness did not necessarily translate into romantic interest.

Cramped from sitting so long in one position, and distracted by her troublesome thoughts, she shifted clumsily and foolishly. The canoe tipped wildly, just as Warren uttered an expletive that turned her complexion pink. She was about to tell him she didn't approve, but before she could open her mouth, the canoe flipped entirely, icy cold water rushed around her, and she found herself trying to kick her way back to the lake's surface.

An arm grabbed her around the waist and held her securely. She relaxed into the embrace and felt a comforting warmth steal through her. What a lovely feeling!

"Are you okay?" Ross's voice was thick with concern.

She shivered again, and this time the reaction had nothing to do with the temperature of the water. "Ross?" Her tone was puzzled. How had he gotten to her so quickly?

"It's me, Katie. Are you okay?"

"Katie!" Warren's voice, edged with angry tension, split the air. "Where the hell are you?"

"Over here," she managed before Ross clamped a hand over her mouth.

"Shut up, Katie. You are not going anywhere with that man."

She sputtered furiously, then realized that the sensation of her lips against his palm was doing wicked things to her insides. Outrage changed traitorously into excitement, and she greeted the sensation with a tiny gasp of pure pleasure. Her legs tangled with Ross's and he took the opportunity to hold her even more tightly, imprinting his hard masculinity onto her softness. Her body yielded all too readily.

"The lady came as my date," Warren said, spoiling the moment. "She'll leave with me."

"Afraid not, pal. If your handling of that canoe is any indication, she'll be risking her life spending another minute with you."

"She's the one who tipped the damn thing over," Warren said, which Katie considered rather unchivalrous of him, even if it was true.

"She probably did it trying to get away from you. What did you do to her?"

Warren loomed closer, and Katie could feel Ross's muscles bunch with tension.

"Ross!" Katie said, yanking his hand away from her face. It drifted down to land somewhere in the vicinity of her right breast. Not somewhere in the vicinity, she corrected herself with a sense of shock. His hand was quite firmly, if accidentally, on her breast, and it felt incredible, even through two T-shirts and a bra. Or maybe it was just the icy water that had made her nipples tighten, she thought hopefully. At any rate, her intention of telling Ross to back out of his argument with Warren got lost in yet another unexpected, fiery sensation.

Unfortunately, Ross seemed to be oblivious to the location of his hand or the melting sensation it aroused. Rather than taking advantage of it, he glowered at Warren, muttered under his breath, shifted his hold on her, and lugged her toward shore in an effort that was ungainly, if gallant. Deprived of the sweet, aching torment of his touch on her breast, Katie found her irritation mounting, fueled by an unfamiliar sense of frustration. His arrogance in assuming that she'd needed rescuing in the first place suddenly infuriated her all over again. She'd had her fill of being smothered in her marriage to Paul.

"Ross! Put me down this instant!"

He complied, and she landed on the grass with a soft thud. He stood there scowling alternately at her and at Warren, who was towing his canoe toward shore. Ross's canoe was being towed in by another boater.

"I'll drive you home," Warren offered, standing before her in soaked clothes, his brown hair matted to his head. He looked considerably less debonair than he had when he'd arrived on her doorstep, but no less disgruntled.

"Thanks, Warren," Katie said, only to have Ross glare at her ferociously.

"You are not leaving with him," he said with an ominous edge to his voice.

"I came with him. I'll leave with him." She met his gaze defiantly. If she didn't make herself understood now, this business of being followed on her dates could go on indefinitely.

"But—"

"Nope. I'm not listening to a word you have to say."

"Dammit, the man's dangerous. You could have been killed out there."

"The canoe tipped over, Ross," she said with what

she considered to be astonishing patience. "I can swim. My life was not in danger. You overreacted."

"You want to go home with him?" Ross asked, amazement written all over his face.

Katie groaned. This wasn't working. "That's not the point."

"Look," Warren interrupted. "I'm not about to get into the middle of some lovers' spat. I told you before, Katie, I'm looking for someone ready to make a commitment. You've already made one."

"I have not," she countered indignantly. She cast a quick, covert glance in Ross's direction and felt an all-too-familiar tingle of excitement. What a fib! She *had* made some sort of odd emotional commitment, and she knew it. She was as involved with Ross as if they'd declared their intentions months ago. Dammitall to hell, why would she do something so stupid? *He* hadn't made any commitment beyond driving her crazy.

So, she thought, where do we go from here? Distance. That was the answer. She had to put some distance between them before she made an absolute fool of herself.

"Let's go home," Ross said. She wasn't sure if he'd been reading her mind or was simply reacting to Warren's departure. Going home was one answer— as long as Ross didn't expect to come in with her. In fact, it might be very nice if they didn't see each other again for about a month. By then she might be ready to deal rationally with this strange new side of his personality.

"Fine. Terrific. Take me home." She stared at Ross with fire in her eyes. "But so help me, Ross Chandler, if you ever come along on another one of my dates, I'm going to have you arrested for harassment."

He grinned at her tolerantly and let her rant on. If she hadn't been shivering in the suddenly chilly air, and if she hadn't left her purse at home, she'd have told him to go straight to hell and taken a cab home. As it was, she got into the car, slammed the door emphatically, and waited while he tied the canoe securely on the roof. She took a certain perverse pleasure in dripping all over Ross's front seat.

On the drive to Katie's house, Ross tried to bring his temper back under control. When he'd seen that canoe tip over, he wanted to kill that guy. Katie hadn't been likely to drown, that was true enough. But she could have been hurt, and the thought of her being injured had made him go all queasy and cold inside.

Even now, she was sitting there dripping wet and shivering, but with her head held high and a defiant gleam in her eyes. She was spoiling for a fight, and sooner or later they were bound to have one. If he had a grain of sense in his head, he'd drop her at her front door and steer clear of her until Monday, when they could have a perfectly civilized discussion about all of this—maybe even a laugh.

Instead, the minute he pulled into the driveway, he found himself cutting off the engine, getting out of the car, and following the trail of water Katie was leaving on the sidewalk. Furious as she was, he was surprised there wasn't steam rising all around her.

Lisa, her hair only a shade lighter than Katie's and her eyes just as big and blue and bright, stood in the doorway and watched their approach. She grinned, then wisely tried to smother it.

"Mom, what happened to you? And Mr. Chandler? Did you two fall in?"

"Good guess," Katie mumbled, wondering how Lisa knew Ross's name. "Get me a towel, would you, Lisa? I don't want to drip on the floor."

"Mr. Chandler, too?"

"I suppose."

Hearing the grudging tone, Lisa shot her mother a quizzical look. Katie grimaced. "Oh, of course. Get Mr. Chandler a towel, too."

The minute Lisa had vanished up the stairs, Katie whirled on Ross. "How did my daughter know who you are?"

Uh-oh. He fumbled for a logical explanation. "She must have seen me at the office or something."

"Lisa hasn't been to the office."

"Oh."

"*Oh* is right. Explain."

"Well, actually, I stopped by earlier."

Katie stared at him, and all of the missing pieces of the day's puzzle clattered down around her. With a little rearrangement, they fell into place. "And I suppose she just happened to mention that I had gone to Green Lake?"

"I was looking for you. I thought maybe we could do something. What was she supposed to do? Lie?"

"Of course not. Where did you find a canoe so quickly?"

"It's yours."

"Mine!" Katie's voice escalated. "Ross Chandler, you are the most conniving, infuriating, outrageous man I have ever known. When are you going to stop chasing me around and interfering in my life?"

"I'm not sure that I can," he said solemnly. Katie

felt a disconcerting little thrill of pleasure scamper along her spine.

"You're a brilliant businessman. I'm sure you can do anything you set your mind to," she corrected.

He shrugged. "Okay, then. Maybe I don't want to."

"Why?"

This time he sighed, and the dark eyes that met hers were troubled. "I don't know."

"I see."

"I doubt it," he muttered as the electricity crackled in the air around them. She wondered if it was the sort that was attracted to water. If so, they were both in danger from several directions. "Umm, Katie?"

"Yes."

"Do you suppose we could take a hot shower?"

Her eyes widened, and her heart thumped wildly. *We? A shower?* Surely he didn't mean . . . not with Lisa in the house, for heaven's sake!

"The sun's gone in again, and I'm freezing," he added for emphasis, and her heartbeat slowed.

"Oh, of course. So am I." She cast a desperate glance at the stairs, then at him. She wanted him to go home. She did not want him in her shower. Her imagination would be swirling with sensual visions for the next three months. Unfortunately, his lips seemed to be turning blue. She couldn't send a man with blue lips home.

"Lisa!" she called. "Where are those towels?"

Lisa ran down the steps. "I was just waiting for a signal."

"A signal?"

"I didn't want to interrupt anything."

"There was nothing to interrupt," Katie said, flushing.

Infuriatingly, Ross winked and said, "Thanks, Lisa."

Katie noted the look that passed between Ross and her daughter. They looked exactly like delighted coconspirators. Oh, hell, she thought. First, Jennifer and Maggie were encouraging an involvement with any available male in Seattle. Now her own daughter had allied herself with Ross. She didn't stand a chance!

"I'm going to take a bath," she snapped. "Ross, you can use the guest bathroom. Lisa will show you where it is. She can throw your clothes in the dryer, if you like."

"That's okay. I have an extra pair of pants and a shirt in the car."

Of course he did, she thought, seething as she stomped upstairs and filled the tub with steaming water and bubbles. Men like Ross probably always carried around a change of clothes. They never knew where they'd be waking up in the morning.

Men like Ross! She sniffed, throwing her soaked clothes on the floor. What a laugh! There *were* no other men like Ross. Not that she'd found so far. But, dammitall, she had every intention of looking for them. It would be nice if the one she found wasn't quite so domineering, though.

When she went back downstairs, she found Ross and Lisa in the kitchen, laughing as they fixed dinner. This was not the sedate, professional Ross of Chandler Electronics or the rakish man-about-town. This was Ross the purely masculine being who could make a woman's breath catch in her throat. Katie's caught and held as her pulse skittered crazily. Ross's damp and tousled hair glimmered with intriguing highlights. He had an apron tied around his waist, a grin on his face, and no shoes. Lisa was accusing him of being all thumbs as he tried to peel the carrots, and he was taking the criticism to heart.

"This is not something I do every day," he complained, just barely missing his thumb.

"So, you're one of those," Lisa said, as Katie listened and watched from the doorway.

"One of those what?"

"One of those male chauvinists like my dad."

Ross scraped the carrot with a vicious gesture that nearly caught his finger this time. "So, your dad's a male chauvinist, huh?"

"Yeah. He thought my mom should do all the cooking and cleaning and stuff."

"And you think that's wrong?"

"If you'd ever eaten her cooking, you'd know it is."

Ross's laughter echoed off the walls, and Katie found herself joining in despite herself.

"Ungrateful brat," she said as Lisa shot her a guilty look.

"Sorry, Mom, but I cannot tell a lie."

"You could fudge a bit. My cooking isn't *that* bad."

"Compared to starvation, maybe not," Lisa said thoughtfully.

"You're terrible," Katie said, but Ross noted she was still laughing. Katie might be lousy in the kitchen, but his impression that she was a terrific mother was still firmly intact. It was obvious she and Lisa had a close, easy relationship.

"Since I'm so awful in the kitchen, does that mean you plan to cook dinner for us tonight?"

"Sure. Most of it is started already. Mr. Chandler's been helping."

Ross noted the calculated gleam in Lisa's eyes as

she grinned impishly up at him. "Why don't you two go have a drink or something?"

Once he and Katie had been urged off to the living room, he settled down in one of the comfortable, oversized lounge chairs and looked around. The room was exactly as he'd imagined Katie's home would be: cheerful, warm, and inviting. The furniture was made for comfort, the colors chosen for their brightness. It would be impossible to be miserable in a room like this, especially with a fire blazing to chase away the Seattle dampness.

And yet, hadn't Katie said that she had been miserable here?

"What are you thinking about?" she asked him now. "You're frowning."

"I was just wondering how anyone could be unhappy here. It feels so cozy."

"Rooms don't make happiness, Ross."

"I suppose not." He stared into the fire, then finally back at Katie. "What would it take to make you happy, Katie?"

She bit her lip and gazed at the floor. After a long thoughtful pause, she said, "That's a hard question to answer. I'm not sure I know."

"What's so hard about it?" Ross asked. "You were miserable before. You must know what it would take to turn that around."

She smiled at him then, a slow, teasing smile that had the warmth of a summer sun. "There are degrees of happiness. A rainbow can make you feel good for a minute. A movie can make you laugh for a couple of hours. A child's hug can give you an instant's joy." Her expression had turned dreamy, and he wondered what she was thinking.

"What else, Katie?" His voice was hoarse as he felt

the tension between them thrum with a sudden awareness. It was an exquisitely sweet tension that had been building for days now, maybe longer.

"A kiss," she said, her gaze meeting his boldly, then faltering.

He leaned closer, his lips ready for just such a kiss, for the heat and sweetness he knew it could yield. "What does a kiss do, lovely Katie?"

Confusion flitted across her face. "It changes things," she said quietly, and moved away, only inches, but it might as well have been a mile.

"Yes," he said solemnly. "It does change things." What, he wondered, would it have changed for them?

Before he could think that through, Lisa announced that dinner was ready. They ate around the kitchen table, and Ross couldn't remember a time when he'd felt so content. It was as if the restlessness he'd been feeling for months, maybe even years, had vanished, replaced by a longed-for sense of peace and family.

The thought caught him by surprise, and he glanced around the table. Lisa was teasing Katie again, and the two of them were laughing, their eyes sparkling.

Katie was different here, too. The warmth he'd always felt around her was there, stronger than ever, in fact. But the crisp edge of professionalism was gone, along with its contradictory hint of vulnerability. This was Katie's natural environment, whether she realized it or not. Maybe she didn't belong in front of a stove or on top of a stepladder with a roll of wallpaper in her hand, but she had an innate ability to turn a house into a home.

Seeing her this way, relaxed and smiling, made

her seem more attractive than ever. A powerful desire to complete the picture, to sweep her into his arms and carry her back up those stairs and make love to her, ripped through him and left his heart hammering in his chest.

A home. That's what had been missing in his life. *His* home.

He glanced at Katie, felt the blood surge through him, warming him. His woman.

Dear God!

CHAPTER FIVE

Dear Feisty,

Just how feisty are you? I like a woman who stands up for herself. Does that mean you're liberated as well? I live in Tacoma, so we're probably too far apart to see each other often, but I'd still like to meet you, and I do have business in Seattle occasionally. Drop me a note with your phone number and I'll give you a call.

—Ben

ROSS CAME UP behind Katie on Monday morning, put his hands on the back of her chair, and peered over her shoulder as she was typing. As his warm breath whispered past her ear, she promptly made three mistakes in as many words.

Ever since Saturday, she hadn't been able to get

him out of her mind. He'd been in the oddest mood when he left—distracted, yet strangely pleased about something. It had unnerved her even more than his appearance at Green Lake, the surprising, disturbing heat of his body next to hers, the gentle gruffness she'd heard in his voice when he'd plucked her from the water, the instant rapport he'd had with Lisa.

"Is that the report I need?" he asked now, trying to swivel her aside so he could see the page clearly.

Katie planted both feet on the floor to keep the chair from turning and leaned forward in what she hoped was an effective if unsubtle attempt to cover up the letter. She looked up at Ross and gave him a wavering smile. "The report's on your desk."

"Then what's this?" he asked, determinedly nudging her out of the way. He read it, then scowled at her. "Not *another* one?"

"Yes, *another* one," she mimicked. She'd rather liked the idea of just sending a letter, instead of calling. It put the ball back in Ben's court. If he wanted to get in touch, he could. If not, she'd only wasted the price of a stamp, and at least she'd done something to counter the disconcerting effect Ross seemed to be having on her all of sudden.

That tender almost-kiss on Saturday had left her feeling strangely empty and far more alone than she'd felt when Paul had walked out. She'd fought the yearning all day Sunday, using clearheaded logic and a marathon, backbreaking effort to rid the yard of fall leaves. It hadn't worked. Her dreams last night, with Ross at the center of every one of them, had been astonishingly sensual, and she'd awakened today feeling more restless than ever.

"Dammit, Katie, I thought we'd settled this," Ross snapped, bringing her sharply back to the present.

"*We* haven't settled anything. It's none of *your* business."

"But the other night—"

"The other night was fun. Period." Dammit, that was all she was going to let it be. She was not going to set herself up for some brief fling with her boss, a fling that would force her to go out on a job hunt when it was over. And it would be over, she had no doubts about that. Love 'em and leave 'em . . . that was just the way Ross was. His marriage must have scarred him deeply, or perhaps that was the way he'd always been, unable to sustain a relationship. The latter was difficult for her to believe, though. She'd witnessed so many signs of his deep sensitivity, of his thoughtfulness. The Ross she knew was capable of caring deeply. He just didn't allow himself to do it.

"It was more than fun," he was insisting now.

She sighed. "Okay. We had a great time."

"Lisa liked me."

"Of course she did. She got to stay up past her bedtime, and you let her win at cards after dinner."

"I did not let her win. She has a terrific knack for poker."

"And that's another thing. I don't think my daughter ought to start getting any ideas about gambling."

Ross's infectious grin made her heart tumble straight down to her toes. "Katie, you worry too much. Playing poker for matchsticks is hardly big-time gambling."

"Everybody has to start somewhere. The next thing I know, she'll want to go to Las Vegas," she grumbled, but there was a twinkle in her eyes.

"You've done it again," he moaned, his expression

bemused. "How do you do it? I started having a perfectly legitimate conversation about your refusal to listen to good advice, and you go off on some tangent about Lisa being headed for a life of crime or something."

"That's because we have nothing more to say on the subject of my dating."

"*I* do."

"Ross! Just because we spent one pleasant, friendly evening together, that still doesn't give you any rights where I'm concerned. You don't hear *me* telling *you* whom to date. I'm your assistant here, not your mother. And," she said with added emphasis, "you are not my father."

Which was certainly true enough, Ross thought as he threw up his hands and stalked out of her office muttering to himself about the perversity of women. You'd think Katie would be grateful that he wanted to look out for her. She'd advertised for a damned Prince Charming. What was wrong with a knight in shining armor? Instead of being pleased about his concern, she was balking like a teenager whose parents were too strict.

But since that was the way she felt, he'd better wise up. If he didn't want her to start resenting him, if he wanted her to confide in him, he was just going to have to learn to keep his mouth shut. However, the whole idea of sitting back and watching while Katie walked into trouble with that sweet, trusting smile on her face was too much for him. They'd probably cart him off in a straitjacket before it was all over.

He got a chance to practice his vow of silence a few days later. He was with Katie, going over a complex new clause in the Simpson contract, when that

Ben person she'd been writing to the other day called. The now-familiar knot formed in the pit of Ross's stomach, and he had a sudden urge to start throwing things, starting with the phone. He clamped his jaw shut so tightly his teeth hurt.

Ross could only hear Katie's end of the conversation, since she smacked his hand every time he attempted to put the call on the speaker phone. When she offered to call the guy back, Ross's brows lifted quizzically. What kind of deadbeat was this guy? Didn't he even want to pay for a long-distance call?

"Katie . . ."

She scowled at him, and he bit his lip again.

As soon as the call ended, with Katie agreeing to meet Ben later in the afternoon for a drink, Ross couldn't help it. He badgered her with questions.

"Why did you offer to call back? Is the guy that cheap?" he grumbled.

"He was at a pay phone. He had to keep hunting for more change. It seemed like it might be simpler for me to call back."

"Why would he be calling from a pay phone?"

"I have no idea. He was on his way from Tacoma to Seattle. Maybe he stopped at a gas station to call. What difference does it make?"

"I don't like the sound of this. He's probably married or in the middle of a messy divorce," Ross said suspiciously, his lips settling into a hard, forbidding line. "He probably doesn't want any record of the call on his phone bill. That must be what he meant when he wrote and asked if you were liberated. He was trying to see if you'd fool around with a married man."

Katie regarded him in astonishment. "You have

the most incredible imagination. Do you hold all other men in such low esteem?"

"No. Just this guy."

"And Warren and Jason and Ken."

Ross glowered at her. "Just let me see the letter again."

"Forget it."

"Katie!"

Her chin tilted defiantly, and her blue eyes flashed. "I said forget it."

He sighed heavily. "Okay, then. At least tell me this: Does he say he's single?"

That seemed to shut her up.

"Well, no," she finally admitted reluctantly. "But none of the others did, either."

"I don't care about the others. I have a really bad feeling about this one. He's married. You are *not* going to go out with a married man."

"Ross, I am only meeting the man for a drink. I'm not starting up a relationship. I'm sure there's a logical explanation for the pay phone. Why are you making such a big deal about it?"

He sighed again. "You already know the answer to that. Because you're a babe in the woods. You need protection. You might just have a drink today, but what if you fall for the guy and then find out he's married? What then? You'll be moping around here, crying all the time. I won't be able to stand it."

Katie couldn't help it. She laughed, sobering only when she realized that Ross didn't think he was being the least bit funny. His scowl was ferocious.

"This is nothing to laugh about," he muttered indignantly.

"Ross," she began wearily, "when have you ever seen me mope?"

"Maybe you've just never been hurt that badly," he replied defensively.

"I had just been through a divorce when I came to work here. If I didn't mope then, I guarantee you that finding out this man I don't even know is married won't depress me."

"Maybe not, if you find out today. But what if you don't find out until later? What will you do then?"

"I'll deal with that when and if the situation arises."

Ross shook his head. "That's not good enough. It's better to be prepared. You've got to take control of the situation. I think you'd better ask him point-blank. In fact, what you need—"

"What I need," she said emphatically, "is a boss who doesn't meddle in my love life."

"It's not meddling to be concerned about a friend."

Friend, she thought dismally. Why had she thought she might be anything more to him? In the back of her mind, she'd been hoping that Ross's fussing and fuming had been spawned by something more than concern. It appeared that hope was foolish. It was probably just as well that she'd been reminded of it. It seemed to be getting more and more difficult to keep it in mind.

"Concern is one thing, but you've gone way beyond that," she complained. "Leave it alone!"

"Where are you meeting him?" he asked, as if she hadn't just told him to butt out in perfectly plain English.

"Oh, no, you don't. You are not coming on this date, Ross," she said, icy sparks glinting in her eyes. "This is *my* date. You get your *own* date."

But Ross suddenly realized he didn't want to get

his own date. He wanted Katie. *That* was what these crazy sensations were all about, he thought in bemusement. He was falling in love with Katie! No, scratch that. He was *in* love with Katie. Head-over-heels, impossible-to-ignore in love.

The possibility had slipped up on him on Saturday, a tiny seed planted at the back of his mind. Now, nurtured by several days of increasing closeness at work, it had blossomed into reality. With the realization came that same urgent desire to take her in his arms and kiss her, then strip away the prim, businesslike suit she had on and make passionate love to her right here in her office. On the sofa. On the floor. Maybe even on the desk, though it looked pretty darn uncomfortable.

Good Lord, he was actually in love with Katie!

Then came the letdown. Katie was only interested in dating a bunch of strange men who obviously weren't worthy of her. Good grief, she'd even prefer going out with a married man to going out with him!

Short of burning the letters, how was he going to get her to stop playing the field and to see him in a new light? Surely, she had sensed the sparks in the air when they were together. How could he make her realize that what they had was special and not just some casual office rapport? If he openly declared himself, she'd probably just toss the declaration back in his face—with class, of course, but it would still be a rejection.

With most women more than willing to meet him halfway or better, and his own interest seldom more than casual anyway, never before had he had to actively pursue a reluctant woman. Surely, though, he could figure out how it was done. A woman like Katie deserved the best. A courtship worthy of

Prince Charming—wasn't that what she'd said she wanted?

Flowers, he decided. Candy. No, better than that. It had to be more intriguing, something she couldn't dismiss or ignore. It had to put all these other guys to shame, especially this Ben, who sounded like a real bounder. He knew men like this, men who cheated on their wives, set up women in other cities, left a trail of heartache. It wasn't going to happen to Katie!

Damn, he wished she'd tell him where she was meeting the guy. It was probably some out-of-the-way dive where Ben wouldn't be recognized. Ross knew he could follow her again, but she would probably call the police as she'd threatened. She was fed up with his meddling. She'd made that plain enough. He ought to just leave it be.

He couldn't do it. At six o'clock, thoroughly disgusted with his inability to take his own good advice, he found himself ringing Katie's doorbell. He was hoping, but not really expecting, that it would be Katie who answered the door.

It was Lisa.

"Hi, Mr. Chandler. Mom's not here."

"It figures," he muttered.

She peered at him with concern. "Are you okay?"

"No. Mind if I wait?"

"Help yourself," she said, gesturing toward the living room. "Want some dinner? I was just about to make mine. Mom said she'd be a little late. She's meeting some guy for a drink."

Ross's expression brightened. "Did she say where?"

Lisa grinned at him impishly. "As a matter of fact, she did. She also said she'd wring my neck if I told you."

His face fell. "I see."

"She didn't say you couldn't wait here, though."

He trailed into the kitchen after Lisa and sat down at the table. He wasn't even aware she'd put a cup of coffee in front of him until he'd absentmindedly picked it up and taken the first sip.

"Lisa, what does your mother like to do?"

Lisa shrugged. "I don't know. The usual stuff, I suppose."

"What sort of stuff? Does she like going out to restaurants?"

Suddenly, Lisa grinned perceptively. "Oh, I get it."

"Get what?"

"You want to take her someplace special."

He chuckled. "You must drive your mother crazy."

"Why?"

"You're very bright."

"She says I'm too smart for my own good."

"A kid can never be too smart," he said. "So, what about the restaurants?"

"I don't think so. At least she and my dad never did that, and since he left, the fanciest place we've been is one of the seafood places on the water over in Edmonds. We didn't even go there for the food. She wanted to watch the sunset." Lisa sat down opposite him and propped her chin in her hand, reminding him of Katie when she was thinking through a problem. "Sometimes she likes to ride the ferry."

"You mean to go to Bainbridge, or out to the San Juan Islands?"

"Oh, it doesn't matter which ferry, 'cause she doesn't care about getting there. She just likes the ride. Sometimes we've taken the ferry all the way to

Victoria, had tea in that fancy hotel, and turned around and come back."

"Anything else?"

"She likes classical music, especially the flute. And she likes to go for walks around Green Lake."

Ross winced at the reminder. "I don't think Green Lake is such a good idea."

"How about Pike Place Market? She loves to wander around down there and poke at the vegetables and stuff. I think she even likes that yucky fish smell."

Ross was beginning to see that courting Katie wasn't going to be like anything he'd ever done before. Ironically, he found that he liked the idea of doing new things with her, things he'd never shared with anyone else. And unless he was wildly off the mark, she'd never done those things with another man. It sounded as though she and Lisa had been their own best pals, the two musketeers.

Now, though, if he had anything to say about it, there were going to be three. The three musketeers. The way it should be.

He was so deep in his own thoughts that he didn't hear Katie come in, didn't notice her gasp of surprise at finding him at her kitchen table, didn't see her advancing on him with fire in her eyes, didn't notice a thing in fact until a purse slapped him in the shoulder and she muttered furiously, "What the hell are you doing here, Ross Chandler?"

He resisted the urge to rub his smarting shoulder, and instead gave her what he hoped was a dazzling, convincing smile. Lisa, he noted, had vanished. The kid had a terrific sense of timing.

"Waiting for you," he said.

"Why?"

"I had a few ideas about what's been happening with Dorian Hayes," he improvised. "I wanted to bounce them off you and see what you thought."

"And these ideas just happened to occur to you after I left the office to meet Ben?"

"Right in the middle of the highway," he said cheerfully.

"You're a lousy liar."

"I'm not lying!" he said indignantly.

She regarded him skeptically, then quietly poured herself a cup of coffee and sat down. "Okay, then," she said at last. "What are your ideas?"

It was a logical question, and Ross had anticipated it. What he hadn't done, however, was come up with an answer. He said the first thing that popped into his head. "Sabotage."

"Sabotage! You think someone is stealing our plans and selling them to Dorian Hayes?"

"Well, it makes sense, doesn't it?"

Ironically, now that he'd said it, he thought the idea might actually have some merit. He couldn't imagine why he hadn't thought of it before. Katie stared at him, her lips pursed thoughtfully. She, too, seemed intrigued with the possibility. "I never even thought of something like that, but you could be right. When did Hayes start beating us on things?"

"About six, maybe eight months ago."

"I can't imagine that anyone who'd been with you a long time would sell you out to the competition. Did you hire anyone new around that time?"

"I don't remember. I'll have to check the personnel records. If it's not someone new, though, it could be someone with problems. Have you heard any gossip about anyone needing money?"

"Nope."

"Keep your ears open, then."

Katie gazed into Ross's eyes, and he felt a familiar heat steal through him. "I'm sorry," she said softly.

"Why?"

"For doubting you. I thought you were here checking up on me again."

Lisa wandered in just in time to hear her mother's comment. She gave Ross a wink as she poured herself another glass of milk and left.

"Nope," he said. "I'm going to try to let you make your own mistakes. Your life is your business." He thought he sounded incredibly noble. Adopting the most casual tone he could manage, he added, "So, how was the date?"

Two pink stains appeared on Katie's cheeks. "Fine," she said tersely.

"Just fine?"

"Okay, it was lousy. Does that make you feel any better?"

Actually, it made him feel terrific, but he was wise enough not to admit it. "What went wrong?"

Katie sighed. "Can't you just leave it alone?"

Ross shrugged. "If that's the way you want it."

"It's the way I want it."

There was a very long pause, an endless silence that Ross had to fill. He couldn't keep his blasted mouth shut. "He was married, wasn't he?"

"With four children and a damn sheepdog," she muttered, then glared at him. "Satisfied?"

He picked up her hand and brushed his lips across her knuckles. "Not especially." He turned the hand over and kissed her palm and felt a shudder sweep through her. "I'm sorry, Katie."

"Yeah," she said. "Me, too."

What Katie was most sorry about, though, was the fact that Ross's lips were on her hand and not on her mouth. If the man didn't wise up and kiss her soon, she might very well die from frustration.

CHAPTER SIX

Dear Enchantress,
*   You intrigue me. With your red hair, I'll bet
you have the most incredible eyes. Blue, probably. What more could any man ask than to
spend the rest of his days beholding such
beauty? The image of you fills my dreams, and
yet you are alone. Why? What are you looking
for from life? Adventure? Romance? I hope
someday to find out.*

KATIE TURNED THE note over looking for a signa-
ture, a phone number, something. There wasn't even
a return address on the envelope.

How odd, she thought, and started to toss the letter into the trash. It had come in the last batch of
mail. There'd been only two letters this time, and

this one intrigued her in a way she couldn't quite explain.

Maybe it was the man's poetic way with words, his attempt to describe her without ever having met her —and in such romantic terms, too. Maybe it was the bold typeface, which suggested a man who'd chosen his typewriter to match a strong, aggressive personality, while his anonymity suggested shyness. It was an alluring combination.

More likely, she was fascinated simply because there was an air of mystery to it. She was just perverse enough to feel an instinctive attraction to a man who wouldn't even identify himself. It appealed to that need she'd felt lately to take more risks, to open herself to new adventures. Admittedly, it also helped to take her mind off Ross for a few minutes.

Whatever the real attraction was, she couldn't bring herself to throw the letter out. She tucked it back into its envelope and put it into her briefcase. Several times during the day, she caught herself wondering about the mysterious man who'd written it, wondering if he'd ever declare himself.

She didn't have a lot of time for such daydreaming, however. She and Ross had spent the morning plotting a strategy for discovering the leak at Chandler Electronics. They were both now convinced that Ross's sabotage theory made sense, that someone was feeding information to Dorian Hayes. She had lists of employees on her desk, along with their employment history, their work areas, and their hours. She'd promised to spend the rest of the day—the rest of the week, if necessary—trying to determine who might want to sell them out and who'd had access to the information that had fallen into Hayes's hands.

She was sketching a layout of the offices when the

piped-in background music suddenly scratched to a halt. Normally, it was so unobtrusive she didn't even notice it, but it was impossible to ignore the horrible screeching sound. Katie stuck her head out the door and spoke to the secretary.

"Paula, what on earth was that?"

"I don't know." Paula shivered dramatically. "If it does it again, though, I'm going out for coffee. I may even take the rest of the day off. The sound gives me the creeps. It reminds me of chalk on a blackboard, and the fact that I failed math because the teacher couldn't write on the blackboard without making that noise."

"I'm not sure I'm following you."

"I couldn't stand the noise, so I had to cut class a lot. As a result, I failed. I had to go to summer school, and I got the same damned teacher. If my parents hadn't threatened me with banishment, I probably would have failed again."

Katie laughed.

A moment later, the music started again. Classical, Katie noted in surprise. Mozart's Quartet in G Major. Her face lit with a smile at the sound of the flutes, and she was transported to a field where she'd spent a wonderful day last summer listening to a chamber-music concert with wildflowers all around and the sunshine brushing her shoulders with a golden heat.

Paula was listening to the music with an expression of astonishment on her face. "When did the boss start going for classical music?"

"What does Ross have to do with this? I thought we paid for some service."

"We do, but he was asking about the music system

this morning. I just assumed he was the one who was in there tampering with the hookup."

Ross suddenly emerged from his office.

"What do you think?" he asked, his eyes flashing excitement.

"It beats 'Fly Me to the Moon'," Paula said.

"I think it's wonderful," Katie added, staring at Ross in utter fascination. This was yet another new side to him. "What brought on the change?"

"Oh, I just thought it was time we had some different music around here. Something a little more high-class." He shot Katie a speculative glance. "Do you really like it?"

"Mm-hm. I love anything with flutes, and the Mozart flute quartets are wonderful."

He nodded in satisfaction. "Good. I just have a tape on now. I'll call the service and tell them we want to switch from easy listening to classical." He turned around and went back in his office, but not before Katie caught the oddly satisfied expression on his face.

Now what on earth did that mean? she wondered. It was strange how close she sometimes felt to Ross, as if she could read his mind, but she still didn't begin to understand him. He was like a crystal twirling in sunlight, constantly changing colors, its brightness elusive and tantalizing.

As much as he had infuriated her lately with his meddling, she had a deep respect for him as a man, for his integrity and values. He was intelligent, witty, sensitive, and, most important of all, he held her in high esteem. He'd given her a break when she needed it, and she had worked her tail off for him ever since to prove that he hadn't made a mistake. His praise and his trust proved that she'd succeeded.

She knew, though, that something had shifted in their relationship over the last few weeks. They'd gone from being respectful business associates to something more, but what? There were strong undercurrents every time they were in a room together, a sexual pull that hadn't been there before. She'd always found Ross attractive, goodness knows, but only recently had she felt this yearning to explore the sensations he aroused in her. Sometimes he looked at her as though the same intense feelings were burning in him, but he'd done nothing about it, and Katie wasn't worldly enough to know how to change that.

She still wasn't sure it was wise to change it, either. It would complicate their excellent working relationship in ways she couldn't even begin to imagine.

It was nearly midnight Friday, after a long week of similar nights and similar longings, when she felt Ross's hands on her shoulders, massaging away the tension. The first touch filled her with contentment as a subtle warmth stole over her. A Bach flute sonata flooded the air with joyous sound, and her contentment deepened.

Ross's touch changed so subtly that at first she wasn't even aware that it had gone from a friendly gesture to a sensual assault. Fingers slid beneath her hair to caress her neck. A new tension came back to replace the one just eased, a different sort of tension entirely, one that was achingly sweet. Lips touched her ear, then a tongue dipped into that shell, sending shock waves rippling through her. Warmth became a white heat that settled low in her abdomen.

In this setting with any other man, she'd have been screaming about sexual harassment. Even now, she thought briefly of protesting, but the feelings were first too tempting, then too demanding. This wasn't just any man, it was Ross... and she wanted more. His touch was everything she had imagined it could be. Tender. Bold. Thrilling.

"Come here, Katie," he whispered, his voice hoarse with longing. "Please."

She was powerless to refuse. No, not powerless. Unwilling. He drew her up and into his arms at last, their bodies separated for an instant by hesitancy, then together, a perfect fit. The kiss... ah, the kiss was something else. Slowly and leisurely, his lips explored, then plundered with a need that took her by surprise. The textures, the taste, the power of that kiss melted any hint of resistance. She was at first astonished, then confused, then lost entirely to sensation.

Her heart beat in tandem with his, far faster than normal, sending the blood rushing to her head, and flames leaping through her veins. A shudder swept through both of them, and then he was stepping back, drawing in ragged breaths, his fingers digging into her arms. There was a raw and urgent hunger in his eyes that stunned her.

Her still-startled gaze was locked with Ross's for an eternity before Katie finally blushed in embarrassment and pulled away.

"I'm sorry," she mumbled. "I don't know what got into me."

Ross shook his head. "No. I'm the one who should be apologizing." He met her gaze evenly. "But I won't. I wanted to do that."

"Why?"

"Because you're a very desirable woman."

She sucked in her breath and eyed him cautiously. "I never knew you thought of me that way."

"These days I hardly think of anything else."

"You're just tired," she said, seeking a justification that wouldn't alter things between them irrevocably, even though her heart screamed that it was too late. "We've been working a lot, and you haven't been cavorting around town with your usual bevy of beauties. I was just convenient. The proximity . . ." Her voice trailed off as he glowered at her.

"No!" he said so adamantly that Katie had to accept that perhaps she was wrong. It had been a while since she'd seen any of those women in the office. True, she and Ross had been working especially hard, but Ross's demanding schedule had never prevented most of those women from dropping by in the past. Was it possible that Ross truly did find her attractive, and that he had lately discouraged visits by his dates?

"Ross, this isn't a good idea. Why don't you call that tall, leggy blonde, the one who always looks as though she could use a good meal? Take her out to dinner."

"At this hour?" he said with amusement.

"I'm sure she'd be delighted to hear from you at midnight or 3 A.M. or even dawn," she said. *I would be,* she added mentally.

As though he'd read her mind, he asked, "Would you go out with a man who called at midnight?"

"If I wanted to see him, I might."

"I don't think so, Katie. You'd probably tell him to take a hike."

"But I'm not like those other women. I'm not so casual, carefree, always ready for a good time."

"No," he agreed. "You're not. That's what makes you so special."

The words stole into her heart, filling it with pleasure. Still she argued, "We have to work together. I think it's better if things stay the same between us. Let's not mess up our working relationship by playing with fire." It was a halfhearted protest at best, filled with logic but empty of conviction.

He knew it, and he grinned at her. "Does that mean you feel the fire, too?"

She couldn't look away from the oddly hopeful glint in his eyes. "Yes," she finally admitted in a soft whisper, her vision suddenly misty with unexpected tears.

Ross beamed, obviously delighted by her answer and unaware of what it had cost her to make it. "Well, now, Mrs. Stewart, I think you and I have some plans to make."

"Plans?"

"How would you like to go on a ferry ride tomorrow? If the weather's nice, we could take along a picnic."

"A ferry ride? Picnic?" She repeated the words in consternation. Ross wasn't the type to spend a Saturday with such simple pleasures. He should be wearing a tuxedo and dining at some elegant restaurant, or jetting down to San Francisco for the day or attending a charity gala.

"If you're worried about the picnic, I'll pack it," he was saying now, a teasing curve to his lips. "How do you feel about cold fried chicken, maybe some deviled eggs, and potato salad?"

It sounded simple and familiar. It sounded wonderful. "You really want to go on a ferry ride and a picnic?"

"Is that so astonishing?"

"Yes," she said bluntly. He chuckled at her wide-eyed expression. "Why, Ross?" She regarded him suspiciously. "Are you just trying to keep me from going on another one of those dates?"

"No. I'm trying to take you on a date myself. I must be out of practice. Usually, my intentions are much clearer."

"But why would you want to take me on a date?"

"So, we're back to that again. I would have thought the kiss made that perfectly clear."

"No," she said. "It only confuses things."

"How?"

"I'm not very sophisticated, Ross. Not like those other women you see. A kiss doesn't necessarily mean I'll land in your bed."

Ross had to work very hard to hide a grin at her straightforward declaration. "Of course not."

"And that doesn't bother you?"

It made him crazy, but he simply shook his head, denying what she wasn't ready to hear: They were going to make love. Maybe not tomorrow, but soon.

First, he had to convince Katie that he, and not any of those jerks she'd been meeting, was the right man for her.

"Ross, I'm not your type. I'm not sophisticated," she repeated, not even hearing him when he muttered, "No. Thank God."

She wasn't sure why she felt this need to talk him out of a date she very much wanted to go on. Suddenly, she was scared—terrified, in fact. These other men hadn't posed any threat to her independence. Ross did, and she knew it. She'd known it for weeks now. Ross was excitement and adventure and challenge all rolled into one. His was a way of life she'd only imagined—the impetuous, carefree lifestyle she'd felt she'd missed. Because of that, he repre- sented the biggest risk of all and, for all of her talk,

she wasn't the least bit sure she was ready to take it.
What if she discovered that the lure of the unobtain-
able was more fascinating than the reality? It would
spoil her dreams. Worse, what if he left her as Paul
had? This time the hurt would be unendurable.

Was she worrying too much again? To her confusion, Ross wasn't exactly plunging her into a whirlwind tour of the high life. He wanted to take her on a
ferry ride, a simple, run-of-the-mill ferry ride. Something she'd done a hundred times. Something she
loved.

"What time?" she said at last. One small step for
the old, brave Katie.

"I'll pick you up at noon. Wear something warm in
case we don't get home until late."

She wore jeans and two T-shirts and tied a heavy
sweater around her shoulders. According to Lisa, she
also had a silly grin on her face.

"So, Mom, what are you and the hunk going to
do?"

"That's no way to talk about Mr. Chandler."

"You think he's a hunk, don't you?" Lisa asked
with feigned innocence.

Katie blushed. "Oh, he's a hunk all right, but it's
not polite for you to say it. What if he heard you?"

"Heard her what?"

Katie whirled around and noted the complacent
grin on his face, the unreadable expression in his
eyes. He'd heard every word, which forced her to go
on the offensive to recapture some sense of control
over a situation that was spinning wildly out of control.

"How did you get in here?" she asked indignantly.
"I didn't hear the doorbell."

"The front door was wide open. You ought to

watch that. You never know what sort of creeps might be around."

"I'll remember that," she said pointedly. Ross grinned back at her, his expression filled with oddly boyish excitement. He clearly wasn't about to let her spoil the day or his mood.

"Are you all set?"

"She's been ready for an hour," Lisa blurted out, and Katie considered strangling her.

Ross's grin widened. "Then we'd better get going before she changes her mind."

Katie followed Ross out the front door and wondered why she felt that her life was about to undergo a change from which she might never recover.

They drove downtown to the ferry in silence, driving the car onto the boat, then going upstairs to the lounge, where Ross bought them each a cup of coffee and found seats by the window. It wasn't the best sort of day for a ferry ride. The sky was gray, the water shrouded in mist. Yet that was the way Katie preferred it.

Ross leaned back in the seat across from her and in sheer fascination watched the delightful play of expressions on her face. She was like a kid at Christmas—or a woman in love—her eyes alight with excitement, her mouth curved ever so slightly into a dreamy smile. She turned and caught him looking at her.

"What are you grinning about?" she asked.

"You. You really do love this, don't you?"

"Don't *you?*"

"I've never really thought about it. I only take the ferry when I need to get across to one of the islands."

"But just look out there. Look at the water, how smooth it is. And the sun filtering through the mist."

She pointed. "And over there, the first sight of land, like Brigadoon rising in the fog. You can believe in enchantment on a day like this."

Ross believed. He believed more than ever that he needed Katie in his life. Katie who could make the simple pleasures so special; Katie who still believed in fairy tales and happily ever after. If only she'd realize that she'd been looking for a man in all the wrong places.

The afternoon was filled with laughter and discovery. They drove to the village of Poulsbo, where even the Dairy Queen had a Scandinavian decor; and Ross told Katie about his trip to Denmark a few years earlier, about the magical world of Tivoli after dark and the outdoor sculpture gardens and avant-garde art at the Louisiana museum, which was housed in a remodeled home that overlooked the sea and drew in the view through huge windows. Even on a dreary, rainy day it was a spectacular setting. The art, on the other hand, had puzzled him.

"In one room there was a big circle of rocks on the floor," he recalled. "I kept wondering if it would still be art if I moved one of the rocks."

Katie appeared intrigued. "Did you do it?"

"Nope. I figured I'd land in jail and then I'd never get to go back to Tivoli to ride the magic carpet."

Her eyes sparkled, the blue far brighter than Puget Sound. "Tell me about the magic carpet."

"It's a ride that looks perfectly innocent. No steep hills like a roller coaster. No wild curves. It's just this flat platform with rows of seats across. Talk about deceptive. The platform moves forward, then back, higher and higher each time. I thought my stomach was going to drop out before the damned thing stopped."

"Lisa would love it."

"What about you?"

She grinned. "I'd like to watch you on it."

He reached over and touched her cheek, a butterfly's touch, soft and gentle. "We'll put it on the agenda."

What agenda? Katie wondered as they strolled along the boardwalk, which edged the waterfront before curving up into an arboretum that was painted bright from the gold and red and orange palette of fall. What was Ross planning for the two of them? She wanted to ask, but she wasn't sure she was ready to hear the answer.

He spread a blanket out in the shade of a huge old tree, settling it so they would have a view of Puget Sound. They ate the promised chicken and eggs and potato salad.

"This is wonderful. How did you learn to cook?" Katie asked, wiping her fingers on a napkin. "The way you grumbled about peeling those carrots, I thought you'd never been near a kitchen."

"Peeling carrots is not cooking," he said loftily. "My mother believed men should be self-sufficient, and she felt that required more than sticking a TV dinner in the oven. My brother and father and I were expected to prepare dinner every Saturday night. At first it wasn't much more than hot dogs and baked beans, but then we started getting into it. It got to be a challenge to prove to her that we could do it. We took turns finding recipes. We developed specialties."

"What were yours?"

"*Coq au vin*, chocolate soufflé, and, best of all . . ." He hesitated, and Katie practically licked her lips in anticipation. "Peanut-butter-and-jelly sandwiches."

"That's my specialty, too," she confessed with a laugh. "Unfortunately, the mere thought of *coq au vin* intimidates me and the only time I tried a soufflé, it fell so dramatically Lisa thought it was some sort of weird cheese pancake."

"I'll show you how it's done. Anyone who can read can cook."

"Not so," Katie protested. "I was a literature major, remember."

"But you didn't want to cook, did you?" Ross teased, reaching over to brush the hair off her face. His fingers lingered to caress her cheeks, which were warm from the sun. He heard her breath catch, saw the pink stain rise to color her complexion. "Wasn't not cooking part of your rebellion, Katie love?"

"What rebellion? I was a model wife."

"On the surface, maybe."

Katie drew her knees up under her chin and stared at the ground, thinking about what Ross had said. Suddenly, she realized it was true. She had tried hard to smother all that impulsiveness that was her nature, but subconsciously she had rebelled in the only way she knew how. She simply hadn't cooked. Not well, anyway.

"I picked a hell of a way to punish my husband, didn't I?" she admitted with a sigh.

Ross shrugged. "It was probably better than fighting with him."

"Not really. That might have cleared the air." She grinned at him. "Do you realize that I have fought with you more in the last few weeks than I did with Paul in all the years we were married?"

"Am I supposed to consider that a blessing?"

"I think so. Without communication, two people don't stand a chance of making a relationship work."

"Is that what we're doing, Katie? Giving our relationship a chance?"

"I didn't mean . . ."

"Don't back away from it," he said gently. "We have a relationship, a good one, based on friendship and trust and respect. I want . . ."

His hand was on her neck, drawing her down until their lips were only a fraction of an inch apart. "I want so much from you, Katie." Their lips met on a sigh, their breath mingled, and she felt that ache beginning to build again, an insistent longing that cried out for fulfillment.

Eyes wide, she gazed at him, caught the uncertainty that warred with desire. She reached for him, and the uncertainty fled, leaving only the desire, the mounting passion that was a thrilling torment. His mouth caressed with the gentleness of heaven. His hands bedeviled her with the fire of Satan. His body, pressing her down against the cool, sweet-smelling grass, covered her with the welcome weight of a blissful reality. This was danger and serenity, excitement and wonder.

It was, she thought, fighting against the tide of her feelings, a mistake.

He apparently sensed her withdrawal before she could speak, before she could move. He knew her so well, better than Paul, better than she herself did. He was so quick to understand, so slow to judge.

"What is it, Katie love?"

"I don't want to be one of your women, Ross."

"You won't be. The others don't matter, don't you realize that? They never did."

"Exactly. How long would it be before I'd join the ranks of the forgotten?"

"Katie, that's not the way it would be with us." ·

"You can't be sure of that."

"You can't be so sure it won't work. What happened to the woman who wanted to start taking risks?"

"Not this one. The cost's too high."

"You'd rather do what I've been doing? Hiding behind a series of meaningless dates?"

"For now."

"I don't believe that's what you really want. I think you want a family again, a man who'll love you and excite you and challenge you."

She sat up and brushed the leaves from her clothes, pointedly avoiding Ross's knowing eyes, not wanting him to read her vulnerability. She had to show him her strength, convince him of her determination to keep things the same between them... even though she hated it, even though she didn't feel one bit strong.

"I'm all wrong for you," she repeated stubbornly. "We're all wrong for each other."

"Katie, that doesn't make sense. We've known each other for nearly a year. We get along. We're friends. We couldn't have a better base for a relationship."

"An office relationship, not a personal one."

"And I'm just supposed to ignore these other feeling I have for you?"

"Yes," she insisted, not saying that she would be fighting them just as hard as he was.

Ross sighed in frustration. He noted the defiant tilt of her chin, the sparks in her eyes that dared him to continue the argument. He saw all of that and decided for once to keep his mouth shut. To his delight, he saw Katie's expression falter, caught the flash of

something in her eyes that just might have been disappointment.

You've won the battle, Katie love, he thought, *but
I'm winning the war.*

CHAPTER SEVEN

Ah, Enchantress,

My dreams have been filled with you. I see you running barefoot through country fields, your red hair curling about your face in a fiery halo. I feel your lips on mine, tasting of wild strawberries. I wonder how much longer we must be apart, and then I remind myself that an anticipation so sweet can only lead to a magical reality. I await the reality with pleasure. Write to me, Enchantress. Tell me your dreams, so I can make them come true.

NO NAME AGAIN, but there was an address this time, a post office box, Katie noted as a wayward shiver of excitement tripped down her spine. She tried reminding herself that the guy could be some sort of nut, but it didn't matter. Even if he were, he had the gentle soul of a poet. He wrote the most exquisitely romantic things, and he wanted to know about her dreams.

What were they? she wondered. Once there had been so many dreams. Once she'd made crazy, improbable plans for her life. But it had been a long time since she'd even dared to dream, much less acted on those dreams.

Once, for instance, she had longed for just this sort of romance—provocative, enticing. Should she write and tell him that? Ross would have a fit. Even Jennifer and Maggie would think she was crazy. Or would they? They were the ones who'd encouraged her to start living again, to be a little reckless. Maybe she should listen to them. Maybe she should remember the days when she'd done things on a whim, when the lure of the sun had been enough to draw her outside, when a whisper of wind had beckoned her and she'd followed, filled with joy. How important was it for her to recapture those days before time and opportunity slipped away? Would a letter to a stranger do it?

"It might-be a start," she whispered, staring solemnly at her reflection in the mirror. "Just write."

And say what?

She could tell him that at fifteen she'd wanted to be an actress, just for the joy of changing characters, that at seventeen she'd wanted to go on an archeological dig, just for the wonder of piecing together bits of an ancient civilization. She could tell him how the thought of visiting far-off places still excited her, how she'd like to ride a camel through the desert to visit the pyramids, or climb a mountain, or maybe even ride the rapids.

There were times, too, when she wanted to throw

caution to the wind and go on wild adventures like Indiana Jones, or be a government agent like television's Mrs. King and get caught up in harrowing escapades with someone as sexy and bold and brave as Scarecrow. Crazy, impossible, daring dreams, especially for a thirty-four-year-old mother.

What was the harm in sharing such imaginings with this stranger? Even if she exposed her innermost thoughts and vulnerabilities, he couldn't use them to hurt her or make fun of her. He had no idea who she was or where she lived. It was like having one of those invisible playmates of childhood or, perhaps, a secret admirer.

She smiled to herself as she recalled how she'd always wished for a secret admirer as a child. Tall and gangly, though, she'd made most boys her age self-conscious. Other girls got dozens of lace-trimmed valentines from anonymous classmates who were too shy to openly declare their affection. She'd only gotten one; and she'd known exactly who sent it, because Barry Francis Harrison, who was a good six inches shorter than she was, had spent the whole day peering at her hopefully from behind his thick, horn-rimmed glasses and chewing on nails that had already been bitten to the quick. Barry hadn't been her idea of a romantic prince, but she'd smiled at him, knowing how it felt to be left out and alone.

Those days were long ago, though. She had a full life now, and no time for impractical thoughts. Whims were for girls. Finally, reluctantly, she put the letter aside. She didn't have time to spend daydreaming about the past or her secret admirer or the future that couldn't be, because Ross was due in exactly twenty minutes to take her out. He'd persuaded her that there was no reason friends couldn't spend an evening together. When she'd regarded him skeptically, he'd returned her gaze with an expression of such innocence that she'd been lured into agreeing without another murmur of protest.

She had no idea what they were doing. He had refused to give her a single hint, other than to suggest that she dress casually. His deliberate mysteriousness had made her pulse quicken in a way that warned her she was living dangerously. It was another coup for the old Katie, but for *her*? She refused to consider the consequences.

She took a fast shower, selected jeans, a silk shirt, and a heavy, hand-knit sweater in a spectrum of autumn colors. She took extra care putting on her makeup. Her hands were shaking so badly when she heard the doorbell ring that she sent a streak of blue eyeliner clear over to her ear. It gave her a whimsical expression, but she doubted if Ross would appreciate it. It took her extra time to scrub it off and repair the damage.

When she finally went downstairs, Ross was helping Lisa with her homework. They were arguing over the solution to a math problem.

"Just let me use the calculator," Lisa pleaded. "That's the easy way."

"Exactly. That's a cop-out. If you rely on a calculator, you'll never be able to do math."

"I won't need to," Lisa said smugly. "I can always carry a calculator in my purse."

Everything about Ross—his stance, his tone—registered indignation. "Do you want to be part of a generation of mathematical illiterates? You'll never get into a decent college. I guarantee they won't let you take along a calculator when you take the college boards."

"It's just one dumb problem," Lisa grumbled.

"If it's that dumb, you can figure it out.'"

She gave him a calculated and incredibly mature look. "If I do, will you take Mom and me to a movie next week?"

"Your mother was right," he moaned. "First, I got you into gambling. Now you're trying bribery. I'm a terrible influence on you."

"Will you take us?" Lisa persisted.

"Yes."

Lisa bent her head to hide what Katie knew perfectly well was a smirk. Math was Lisa's best subject. She'd been making straight A's since first grade. She no more needed a calculator to solve this problem than Einstein would have. Katie ought to have been angry with Lisa, but she wasn't. She couldn't be, because Lisa was so clearly happy, so delighted to have someone other than Katie express an interest in her schoolwork. The sight of Lisa and Ross with their heads together bent over the paper created a sudden warm glow in the pit of her stomach. Paul had never helped Lisa with her assignments. It was as though he didn't expect his daughter to make use of her mind anymore than he'd expected Katie to use hers.

"I see you've just become another victim of Lisa's manipulative skills," Katie said lightly. Ross caught the twinkle in her eyes and shrugged helplessly.

"What can I say? The Stewart women have me wrapped around their fingers."

"In that case, can I get you to tell me where we're going tonight?"

"Afraid not."

"Would a bribe work?"

"That all depends," he said slyly. "What did you have in mind?"

Katie felt a familiar spark of desire flare into a full-grown blaze. "Never mind," she muttered, heading for the door. "One of Lisa's fresh-baked brownies can't compete with what you're thinking."

"And I thought you were brave and bold as well as beautiful," he taunted as he followed her.

"Not that brave. Besides, it'll be interesting to see if I can conquer my tendency toward impatience. I'll just wait until we get wherever we're going."

She waited, filling the time by drumming her fingers on the car seat, which apparently made Ross just as nervous as she was. Eventually, he reached over and grasped her hand in his.

"Enough," he said, flashing her an insouciant smile. "We'll be there shortly."

"What's the big deal about keeping it a secret?" Katie grumbled, sounding every bit as bad as Lisa. "Were you afraid I wouldn't come if I knew where you were taking me?"

"No. I wanted to surprise you. I saw on some TV talk show that surprises keep a romance fresh."

"We're not having a romance," she reminded him. "You promised to forget all about that. We're just friends. You even said I'd be doing you a favor by going along tonight."

"And you are. I've never been to something like this before. You're going to keep me from making a fool of myself."

"Ross, you could dance with a lampshade on your head in the middle of Pioneer Square, and women would think it was the newest rage. You're not the type who looks foolish doing anything."

As she mentioned Pioneer Square, a restored section of old downtown, they turned into the area, and Ross parked in the first available space.

"I hope you don't mind walking. It's only a couple of blocks."

He tucked her arm through his, and they strolled along the street, peering into cafés and shops that catered to an upscale clientele with rare antiques and extravagant hand-knit clothes. As he caught a glimpse of their reflection in the store windows, he saw that they made a handsome couple. A *couple*. He turned the word over in his mind. It sounded good. It sounded right. He was going to do everything in his power to see that it came true.

At the corner of First Avenue and Main Street, he turned her toward the entrance of the Elliott Bay Book Company, watching her expression for the first signs of excitement. He wasn't one bit disappointed. Her lips curved up and her blue eyes sparkled.

"The reading," she said softly. "You brought me to hear the poetry. How did you know?"

"I'd like to claim omniscience, but I'm afraid I can't. You've been talking about it for the last week, and you left that newsletter lying on your desk. I figured it might be a clue."

"I didn't think you were paying any attention."

"Katie love, I always listen to what you say."

"You always read my mail is more like it," she said dryly. Then her brow creased with a worried frown. "But won't you be bored?"

"Why on earth would you think that? I enjoy poetry, even though I've never come here to listen to an author read before. And even if I hated it, it would be worth sitting here for days just to see the glow in your eyes. You get so much enjoyment out of life, it makes me feel good just to watch you."

Impetuously, Katie stood on tiptoe and kissed him. It was only a casual brush of her lips across his, but it was enough to set his heart hammering and make him wonder what other tortures she was likely to devise to drive him mad with longing. Friends! Heaven help him! How long would he be able to maintain this charade?

"Come on," she urged, tugging on his hand, her fingers curled trustingly around his. "We have some time. Let's look around."

The Elliott Bay Book Company was a favorite gathering spot for Seattle yuppies. Not only was its stock of books extensive and more diverse than the franchise booksellers, it also had an impressive collection of prints and posters from art exhibits around the country. The whole atmosphere was designed to cater to those who had a love of books, and the arts. Ross often came here on Sunday mornings to sit in the coffee shop downstairs with a newspaper or a favorite book, sharing his table and conversation with perfect strangers who were also drawn by the friendly setting.

Katie suddenly dropped his hand and began poking through the collection of poetry.

"What are you looking for?"

"I want a book by the man who's reading tonight. I'll get his autograph and give it to Lisa for her birthday."

"They had a whole display by the cash register. I noticed it as you were dragging me past."

When Katie had made her purchase, they went downstairs, bought two cups of espresso, and joined the others who were waiting for the poetry reading to begin. The author, a native of the Pacific Northwest, had brown hair that brushed his shoulders, a body that was lean and taut and rugged in jeans and a plaid wool shirt, and a voice that was low and soothing. Katie appeared to be entranced.

Fighting yet another ridiculous but all-too-familiar surge of jealousy, Ross took her hand and held on possessively. For the longest time, he wasn't one bit sure she even noticed. Finally, though, after a particularly lovely poem about the inspiring beauty of Mount Rainier, she turned to Ross, smiled, and squeezed his hand. It was a small gesture, but it was enough.

For now, he reminded himself. One step at a time. Any faster and he would scare her off. He wondered if he would survive the torment.

When the reading was over, Katie got his autograph. To Ross's relief, her attitude toward the writer was straightforward and pleasant. There was no awe, no spark of personal interest, even though the man's speculative gaze traveled over her with warm appreciation.

"What would you like to do now?" Ross asked. "Would you like to stay here for another cup of espresso and a snack, or would you rather go somewhere for a drink?"

"I'd like to stay here. I don't want to lose the mood. This place is very special." The blue of her eyes darkened to indigo and danced with sparkling lights. His heart lurched, and he felt a tightening in his loins. He wanted to make her this happy every night for the rest of their lives.

"Then you go find us a table, and I'll get our coffee," he said, settling for the attainable, since she had so determinedly put the future out of reach. "Would you like anything else?"

"Carrot cake, if they have it."

While Ross went up to the counter, Katie found a

table in a corner and sat down, taking out the book she'd bought for Lisa and studying the inscription the author had written.

"May you always share my love for beauty."

Here was yet another man, like her secret admirer, who had a way with words and who took a special joy in beautiful things. Could Ross appreciate that sort of thing as she did, as she suspected her mysterious correspondent would? He had seemed to be enjoying himself. Every time she had glanced at him, he had been smiling, though she had a feeling he'd been paying more attention to her than he had to the reading. Her expression softened at the memory. But she didn't dare to believe that Ross could fall for her and make it last. Friendship—that was all he claimed to be asking of her, and all she was prepared to risk.

When he took her home, he walked with her to the front door, declining her invitation to come in for more coffee.

His fingers tangled in her hair, brushing the curls behind her ears, then drifting along the curve of her jaw. A shiver raced down her spine as she anticipated his kiss. Her lips parted and she waited, every fiber of her being tensed and anxious. Her blood pulsed at a lover's tempo.

"'Night, Katie love," he said softly, and was suddenly gone, leaving her confused and unfulfilled and more determined than ever not to mistake friendship for love.

"You asked for it," she muttered. "He's just following your rules." Knowing that he cared enough to give her what she wanted was small consolation.

Inside, sitting at the kitchen table with a glass of milk and still fighting what she knew in her heart was a losing battle against her growing attraction to Ross, she wrote to her admirer, talking about her fears, spinning out her dreams. When she went to bed at last, she was smiling, trying to conjure up an image of the mystery man, a man who seemed to promise all the things an elusive, uncommitted Ross couldn't give. Asleep, though, she was less successful in banishing Ross from her mind. It was his face, his touch, that made her smile, that made her wake with her flesh hot and then left her feeling an aching emptiness when she reached out for a man who wasn't there. So much of the time, though, in the days that followed, Ross was there for her, warming her with a look, teasing her to laughter, stirring her with the most casual caress.

A week later, as promised, he took Lisa and Katie to a movie. Lisa had chosen one of those teenage caper films, which was playing at Harvard Exit on Capitol Hill. They bought popcorn and homemade cookies at the tiny refreshment stand in what had once been the foyer of the old house, now converted into a theater. The lobby boasted a piano, and tables were set up for chess and checkers to amuse those waiting to get in.

"Come on," Ross challenged Katie, his eyes gleaming with devilment. "Try to beat me at chess."

She grinned back at him. "What do I get if I win?"

"It won't happen."

"In that case, you won't mind making a truly outrageous bet, will you? Perhaps a ferry ride to Victoria?"

"Why not a cruise through the Hawaiian Islands?" he suggested innocently.

"That's *too* outrageous."

"It's my bet," he reminded her. "If I win, we go to

Hawaii." He glanced at Lisa. "The three of us." Lisa's face lit with a grin. "If you win, we go to Victoria."

"I can't afford to take us to Hawaii."

"I pay either way."

"That's not fair. I think there's a flaw in this, but I can't quite figure out what it is."

"Just go for it, Mom," Lisa encouraged. "It sounds to me like you win either way."

The chess game started slowly with Katie cautiously moving a pawn forward one space. By the time the movie was ready to start, Ross had captured four of Katie's pieces and was holding her king in check. A frown furrowed her brow as she concentrated totally on the board.

"Mom, the movie's starting."

"You go ahead, honey," she muttered distractedly. "We'll be here."

"You're not going to go?"

Ross glanced up at Lisa. "Do you mind sitting by yourself?"

"Heck, no. I saw a couple of my friends go in. I can sit with them."

"Then go on. Your mother and I will wait for you out here." He grinned at Katie. "Unless she makes a wrong move in the next sixty seconds. Then we'll join you."

"Go to blazes, Ross Chandler," Katie retorted without looking up from the board.

He shrugged. "I guess we'll still be here."

Lisa flashed him a dazzling conspiratorial smile, and went into the theater.

"So, Katie love, what's your move?"

"I'm thinking."

"Don't think too long. My bishop has an itchy trigger finger. He's been after that king a long time."

Katie moved out of harm's way, and twenty minutes later had Ross's king in check. She smiled smugly. "So there."

"Ungrateful wench. I bring you out for a night on the town, and that's the way you repay me."

"Night on the town?" she said dryly, and glanced around the now-deserted lobby. "We could have done this at home."

"That's true, but Lisa wouldn't have gotten to see her movie."

Her brows shot up, and she gave him a startled glance. "You planned this?"

A guilty flush rose in his cheeks. "Do you mind? I'm all for togetherness, but I couldn't bear the thought of watching that film."

Katie laughed. "Frankly, neither could I."

"Then we all got what we wanted, didn't we?"

"Not exactly," she said, her gaze darting toward the chessboard. "I expect to put your king in checkmate in another couple of moves. Then I will have everything I want."

"Humph!"

Katie won the game and the trip to Victoria. Not even to herself would she admit that she was just the tiniest bit disappointed that they wouldn't all be going to Hawaii.

Hawaii, with its blue skies, sultry breezes, and lush surroundings, would be far too dangerous an environment for the two of them, even with Lisa along as a chaperon. She and Ross would no longer be just friends in Hawaii. She was as certain of that as she was of the sweet, tormenting ache in her abdomen that seemed never to go away these days. In Hawaii, they would lose themselves to their senses, allowing the now-forbidden touches from which there could be no retreat. In Hawaii, there would be slow, sensual lovemaking and heated, urgent sex. Just thinking about it made passion stir in her, smoldering, then raging out of control. It was like the awakening of a volcano, awesome and alluring and frightening all at once.

Hawaii was the entrancing dream, Victoria the reality. Life, she tried to tell herself, was better, if you never lost sight of what was real. She wasn't sure if she believed that anymore, wasn't even sure who she *was* anymore.

"What's on your mind, Katie love?"

"I'm just trying to figure out who I am."

"Heavy thoughts for a night like this. Did you come up with any answers?"

She made a wry grimace. "Not a one."

"What are the choices?"

"They seem to be all muddled up," she said, thoughtfully biting her lower lip. Her brow was knitted by a frown. "Way back, I was unpredictable, a real romantic dreamer. Then I got married, settled down, became responsible. I feel as though I've lost something precious."

"Was it marriage and responsibility that were so bad?" he asked gently. "Or was it that particular marriage? Maybe Paul Stewart was simply the wrong man for you. Relationships take on different configurations depending on the two people involved. What you and Paul had—or didn't have—won't be the same as what you might find with someone else. Don't give up on marriage just because of one mistake."

"Isn't that what you did?"

"For a while," he conceded. "Until I figured out what went wrong."

"What *did* go wrong?" Katie asked curiously. "You've never told me."

"Jaclyn convinced me I was incapable of making a commitment. She asked for a divorce. For several years now, I've been living my life as though what she'd said were *true*."

An odd excitement stirred Katie's blood. "You sound as though you think she might have been wrong."

"She was. I was as commited to her and that marriage on the day of the divorce as I was on our wedding day. She was the one who wanted out. She just wasn't brave enough to take responsibility for it, so she cast the blame on me. I was fool enough to listen, but no more. I know now who I am, and what I believe, and I believe more than ever in love and family and wedding vows. You'll figure out who you are, too. Just give it some time and open your heart."

There was an intensity in Ross's voice and a soul-shattering fire in his eyes that made Katie go weak. When he talked like this, she could almost believe, too; but did she dare? Could she allow herself to fall in love with a man who wanted the very thing she feared most? Truthfully, though, did she even have a choice any longer?

She was relieved when the movie ended and Lisa joined them again. It allowed her once more to put physical, if not emotional, distance between her and Ross. Retreat. Safety.

She looked into his eyes, caught the knowing sparks, the blazing desire that he no longer made any pretense of hiding, and wondered if she'd ever be truly safe again. More frightening still was the realization that she was no longer sure she wanted to be.

CHAPTER EIGHT

My Enchantress,

I received your letter. You can't imagine what it meant to me. You are just as open and honest as I'd hoped. I feel I know you better already. It seems you're a bit of a daredevil. I, too, think it would be exciting to go on an African safari. Let's do it. I'm not so sure about the mountain climbing in Tibet, but I'm game if you are. I've picked out the perfect fountain for us to wade in. I hope you haven't met some other man who will keep us from spending the rest of our lives together doing the unexpected and going wherever our impulses lead us. I live for that moment, and I hope you are starting to as well. Every day will be filled with magic and excitement as long as we're together.

THE LETTER HAD COME to the office yesterday, accompanied by roses, beautiful long-stemmed yellow roses that had filled the air with a glorious perfume and Ross's eyes with a speculative glimmer. He hadn't said a word, though. Not one word. His refusal even to acknowledge the flowers left Katie feeling vaguely let down and irritable.

She'd brought the letter home with her and read it again and again this morning, trying to boost her morale. It wasn't working. She folded the letter finally and tucked it back into its envelope with a sigh.

The letter had promised excitement, reminding her of all the things she felt her life had been missing. She gazed at the stack of laundry waiting to be ironed and thought of the Taj Mahal. She scowled at the dishes piled in the sink and envisioned a coral reef in the Caribbean. Then she sighed. She could use a little excitement about now. Surely there were things she could do that would be more thrilling than looking at her reflection in a clean plate or watching the wrinkles disappear from the no-iron blouses that never seemed quite neat enough when she took them from the dryer.

She had an hour before she was due to meet Jennifer and Maggie for lunch. She paced the house restlessly. She ought to do the ironing or the dishes or at least straighten up the living room. There were photographs all over the place. Ross had been over for dinner the night before, and Lisa had insisted on showing him all the family albums. Naturally she'd been too tired to put them away.

Katie smiled as she thought of Ross's astonishment when he'd seen the yearbook shot of her as the leading lady in *South Pacific*.

"You can sing?"

"I can carry a tune," she said dryly. "There's a difference."

"But you had the lead—you must have been good. Sing something for us."

"No way," she said, shaking her head.

"Come on, Mom. I'll even play the piano." Since Lisa rarely volunteered to practice her piano lessons, Katie had finally agreed. She'd sung "I'm Gonna Wash That Man Right Out of My Hair," an appropriate choice considering her determination to keep Ross at arm's length. He seemed to take some sort of perverse pleasure from her selection. Kissing her soundly when she was finished, he had murmured something in her ear that sounded like, "Not a chance."

The three of them had spent the rest of the evening singing together, collapsing in giggles when Ross and Lisa had gone through an exuberant, if slightly out-of-sync piano duet of "Chopsticks," followed by "Heart and Soul."

Time and again, Ross had caught Katie's eye and smiled in that special, captivating way that turned her living room into an island for two that was every bit as romantic as Bali. While Lisa played, he had stood close to Katie, his arm around her waist, his fingers resting on her hip. Katie had been conscious of the casual nature of the touch, even more conscious of her own wildly intense response to it. If Ross was aware of her tension, he didn't show it. He certainly didn't take advantage of it. When it was time for Lisa to go to bed, he, too, said good night and was gone, once again leaving Katie frustrated and filled with an aching emptiness.

If Ross was playing some sort of cat-and-mouse game with her, he was winning. What concerned her more was that he might not be playing a game at all. Perhaps he'd simply found with Katie and Lisa a surrogate family to share warmth with him without making the demand for a commitment. Yet only days ago, he'd said he was ready to make a commitment... to someone, perhaps not necessarily to her. She'd tossed and turned all night wondering about it.

Now, glancing at the clock on the kitchen wall, she realized she'd spent the whole morning daydreaming about it as well. The blasted ironing would still be there when she came back from seeing Jennifer and Maggie.

Unfortunately, her mood didn't vanish during the drive to the restaurant, either.

"Katie, what's wrong?" Jennifer asked after taking a good look at her. "You seem distracted."

She sighed heavily. "I'm not distracted. I'm confused."

"What about?"

"The way I'm feeling these days. I'd almost rather have the flu."

Maggie peered at her over the top of her menu, which she'd been reading like a starving woman. Maggie had been on a diet for the last three days, and they never should have brought her to an Italian restaurant, Katie decided. She was practically drooling as she read every item on the menu aloud, lingering over the mouth-watering descriptions with enough emotion in her voice to do a highly successful commercial for the place.

Still, she managed to drag her attention away from the list of pasta long enough to ask perceptively, "Katie Stewart, are you finally attracted to one of these men you've been meeting?"

"Two, actually."

"Two!" Both women stared at her in astonishment.

"I know it's beyond your wildest expectations, but one of them didn't even send me a letter. I found him on my own."

"Explain," Jennifer demanded.

"Can't we order first?" Maggie pleaded, her curiosity having been temporarily sated while her hunger was still out of control.

"Maggie, your stomach can wait," Jennifer chided. "This is important. Talk, Katie."

Katie explained about her growing attraction to Ross.

"He's been absolutely wonderful to me—considerate, fun, protective. He's not at all the rake I'd expected. He fixed dinner for us last night. And on Wednesday we went to a movie at Harvard Exit and wound up playing chess in the lobby. We never did see the movie. What we do isn't all that exciting, but somehow he makes it seem that way. Does that make any sense?"

Jennifer was nodding sagely. "It does to me. You're falling for the guy. When you're in love, everything you do seems special."

"That's what I thought," Katie admitted ruefully.

"Why do I have a feeling there's a *but* at the end of that sentence?" Maggie said.

Katie sighed. "There is."

"Are you crazy? Why?"

"I've been getting these letters."

"Of course you have. We've seen them."

"Not these, you haven't."

"You've been holding out on us?" Jennifer demanded indignantly. "Why?"

"I wanted to keep these to myself."

"I can't deal with all this intrigue on an empty

stomach," Maggie said emphatically, and gestured for a waiter. When they'd all placed their orders and she had a breadstick in her hand, she said, "Okay, go on now. What about these letters? Who are they from?"

"I don't know. He never signs them."

"You've had more than one?"

"Three so far. It's so strange. Even though the man hasn't identified himself and I can't even talk to him, I feel this bond with him. Is it possible to be attracted to blue stationery?"

"You can't afford the years in analysis it would take to figure that out," Jennifer retorted. "Stick with Ross. He's flesh and blood."

"Is he ever!" Maggie said enthusiastically.

Katie shot her an incredulous look. "How do you know?"

"I was on my way over one night when he was arriving on your doorstep. I kept right on driving."

"If you kept on going, then how do you know he is so good-looking?" Jennifer demanded.

"Well, I did slow down just a little."

"And how did you know it was Ross?"

"I called as soon as I got home, and Lisa told me."

"I'm going to have to speak to that kid," Katie said with a groan. "She's got a big mouth."

"She likes Ross, too."

"So," Jennifer said, "that's three votes for Ross. Katie, don't even think about those anonymous letters. If you get another one, throw it out."

"But this other man is offering all the things I've always wanted. He even wants to go on a safari with me. Six months ago, I thought that was the kind of man Ross was, but it turns out I had it all wrong. He's perfectly content to stick around home. He's coming over next Saturday to cut the grass and help me rake leaves, and on Sunday we're taking the ferry to Victoria. He's so . . . normal."

"If that sparkle in your eyes is any indication, normal can't be all that bad."

"But it's not what I was looking for. You two wrote the ad. You know what I wanted."

"What you thought you wanted—what *we* actually thought you wanted," Jennifer corrected. "Sometimes your heart has other ideas. Listen to it," she advised. Maggie was too busy eating her pasta to comment. She just nodded.

For the next week, Katie was able to follow their advice and forget about the letters. Every time Ross stepped into her office, the tension between them built. He was carefully distant, though the look in his eyes practically seared her with its intensity. Not only did it make her forget all about the letters, it practically made her forget her own name. When their hands accidentally brushed, she felt the vibration all the way down to her toes. She was worse than a teenager embroiled in a fatal case of first love.

By Saturday, when Ross showed up to work in the yard in an old pair of jeans that were molded to his body in a way that was just this side of indecent, Katie had trouble keeping her mind on raking leaves. She'd made a decision. All that was left was finding the courage to follow through. More than once Ross caught her leaning on her rake, her eyes following him, her breath caught in her throat.

"I'm not paying you to stand around and gaze at the scenery," he taunted.

"You're not paying me at all," she reminded him.

"True." His eyes skimmed over her, lingering where her T-shirt skimmed over her breasts. The shadowed nipples seemed to tighten under his gaze.

Her instantaneous, helpless reaction made his pulse race and his control slip. He ought to be pushing the lawn mower around the yard until he was ready to drop in exhaustion. Instead, he turned off the motor.

"Why don't we both take a break?" he suggested. "I could use a beer. It's hotter out here than I thought."

He didn't explain that what was stirring the heat in the two of them had nothing to do with the late-afternoon temperature—which was sixty degrees— or the activity, which was hardly that strenuous. A beer might be able to get his mind off that puzzled little look that came into Katie's eyes every now and then when she was expecting a kiss he didn't deliver. It might also keep his hands off her.

When she came back with the beers, they sat down on the back steps.

"Ross, can I ask you a question?" she asked, her voice tentative, her eyes focused on the ground. He wanted to hold her hand, to give her confidence. He kept his hands to himself, clutching the beer can so tightly it was a wonder it didn't crush.

"Sure," he said, still playing the scene as casually as he could, though his palms had grown sweaty and his throat was dry. He took a long swallow of the beer.

"Why haven't you kissed me?"

The beer went down the wrong way, and he practically choked. He stared at her, eyes wide with astonishment. "What did you say?" he asked, when he'd stopped sputtering. It was the last thing he'd expected to hear come out of Katie's mouth. Maybe Lisa had written the script for her.

This time she gazed directly into his eyes, and he swallowed nervously. "Why haven't you kissed me?"

she repeated with touching bravado. It was the attempt at bravery that undid him, the uncharacteristic boldness edged with vulnerability. He wanted to kiss her right then, but a kiss would lead to more than either of them had bargained for. He settled for answering her, for entering into a discussion about something that adults simply didn't discuss. If they wanted to kiss, dammit, they acted on that impulse, they lived with the consequences.

Unfortunately, the consequences of kissing Katie were so complex it would take a team of psychologists to unravel them. The alternative was to talk. So Ross talked—or at least he tried to.

"Well . . ." he began. He cleared his throat. He met her gaze, blinked, looked away, and finally back again. "You made it pretty clear that you thought we should just be friends." He swallowed with difficulty. "For now," he amended.

"Friends kiss," she said, a smile suddenly playing about her lips. The devilish nature of that smile did not escape Ross. Eve had probably smiled at Adam exactly like that, and look at the trouble the two of them wound up in. *Friends kiss*, the woman said. Of course they do. On the cheek. A nice, innocent little peck on the cheek, maybe even accompanied by a warm hug.

"Not the way I want to kiss you," he muttered. "Not the way we kissed before."

"Then you do still want to?" she said with what sounded like a sigh of relief.

He felt the blood stir in his veins. Another five minutes of this conversation, and he was going to be in a very embarrassing position. No man, however saintly his intentions, had enough control to weather a situation like this for very long. "Katie, do we have to talk about this?"

"I think so. Why? Does it bother you?"

"It's driving me crazy," he admitted.

"Oh," she said softly, but the amused sparkle in her eyes was brighter than ever. "I don't mind not talking about it, if—"

"If what?" he said, his voice tight with tension.

"If we just do it."

"You mean kiss?"

"Yes."

"Oh, God," he moaned, putting down his can of beer and drawing her into his arms. He held her lightly, trying to bring his racing pulses under control. He was not going to kiss her, though, even if it ruined her self-esteem. Better that than involving her in a relationship she'd repeatedly said she wasn't prepared for.

"Well?" she prodded. "Are you going to kiss me or not?"

He sighed heavily. So much for good intentions. "I'm going to kiss you," he murmured.

His lips slanted across hers, coaxing them apart, tasting the cool beer, reveling in the feel of silk. Katie sighed happily and his tongue invaded her mouth, searching for the sweetest nectar, stirring their blood until both of them knew that this time a kiss would never be enough.

"Oh, God," he whispered again, his hands sliding down her sides, then around to cup her breasts. They filled his hands, the tips hard against his palms. Katie snuggled toward his touch like a sleek and sensuous cat that knew how to abdicate its usual independence for the fleeting alternative of pure pleasure. Was that all Katie was doing?

He tried to draw away, to stop before it was too late, but she clung to him, her hands skimming along his spine, then kneading in a pattern of incredible torment.

"I thought you only wanted a kiss," he murmured huskily.

"I was wrong," she said. "It's not enough."

"But, Katie—"

"Sssh. Don't talk. I want you to love me."

"Bad idea." It was a noble statement.

"Don't you want to?"

"Of course I want to."

"Well, then . . ."

Eve provoking Adam again. Nobility took a nose-dive, replaced by practical considerations. A temporary cop-out at best. "What about Lisa?" he asked.

"She's staying with a friend."

There was a low moan in Ross's throat, and he managed to untangle himself from Katie's caressing hands. "Wait."

"I don't want to wait. I want to be impulsive for once in my life, to do what feels right this minute."

"Katie love, I don't want you to have regrets. Not today. Not ever."

"I won't, Ross. There won't be any regrets." She gazed at him, eyes shining. "No matter what."

A part of Ross wanted to refuse, tried desperately to remember . . . remember what? That what he wanted with Katie was forever, not for an afternoon. But he wasn't strong enough to say no, not when he wanted to make love with her just as much as she wanted him to.

Katie needed to blot out all thoughts of mysterious strangers and wild adventures. She needed to discover if the wildest adventure of all could be right there in Ross's arms.

"Inside, Katie," Ross was saying as he lifted her in his arms and cradled her against his chest. She buried her face in the warm curve where shoulder met neck, breathing in the strong male scent of him, her lips pressed against flesh that was warm and damp. Ross was real. Ross was here. Ross filled her senses, overwhelmed her.

"Where to?" he said when he reached the hallway. "The living room? The bedroom?"

"Both of them," she said. "Maybe even the kitchen, too."

"My God," he moaned as Katie, laughing, pointed up the stairs, then directed him to her room, glancing around and trying to envision it through Ross's eyes. She had redecorated in the last year, getting rid of the dull, drab colors that reminded her of her marriage, and replacing them with bright yellow that made the room seem sunny on the dreariest Seattle day. Turquoise throw pillows added to the cheerful decor, and sheer curtains fluttered in the cool breeze, letting in light and garden scents. The queen-sized bed was the room's centerpiece, and gazing at it, Katie had a fleeting attack of nerves.

What in God's name was she doing? She had boldly invited Ross up here, practically seduced him, in fact. What if he was only making love to her out of pity? What if he thought the poor divorcée needed male companionship and he was providing it only to keep her from having her fling with some man she barely knew? She thought of all that and then she looked into his eyes, which were filled with tenderness and a dazzling display of fire and yearning. Her doubts vanished.

Ross placed her gently on the bed, then stood and stripped off his shirt. His bare chest was matted with sweat-darkened whorls of hair. His fingers fell to the snap on his jeans as Katie's fascinated gaze followed.

"No," he said suddenly, leaving the snap untouched as Katie's heart sank. He grinned at her. "Don't look so disappointed, Katie love. I'm just going to let you do the honors. I want you to be sure every step of the way. If you change your mind, we stop."

"I won't change my mind."

He touched a finger to her lips. "You have before."

"I know, but I'm wiser now."

"Oh, really?" His tone was amused. "And what brought on this wisdom?"

"The realization that I'm . . ." She hesitated under the heat of Ross's gaze. "That I care about you." A flicker of something that seemed to be disappointment transformed his features, then vanished just as quickly.

"Are you sure you're not just trying to fill a void in your life?"

"Not the way you mean. I enjoy sex and I've missed it, but I'm not so desperate that I'd hop into bed with anyone to fulfill myself. It wouldn't work, anyway. I'd still feel empty afterward."

Ross heard what she said. And what she didn't say. It was the latter that made his heart fill with joy as he ran his hands along the length of her, like a sculptor anxious to know every perfect curve of his masterpiece. The gentle swell of a breast; the deliciously rounded buttocks; the smooth, flat stomach; the tantalizing dip between tiny waistline and flaring hip; the sleek line of a leg; then back again, feeling her tremble as each touch became more intimate. Her skin burned with fire, and her eyes, at first cautious and vulnerable, darkened with the blaze of passion. Indigo. Sapphire. Every blue of the spectrum tempted him, encouraged his touch.

He lifted her T-shirt over her head, his eyes drawn to the breasts that filled the lacy, revealing cups of her bra. His fingers played along the edge of the lace, skimmed the peaks of her breasts and moved on, resisting the arch of her back that would have brought her firmly within his grasp. His intention was to tease and torment, but also to go slowly, to give her time to adjust to each sensation, time to flee, even though he felt as if he'd die if she did.

Katie must have sensed his caution, because she grew more bold. Her lips were everywhere—on his neck, his forehead, his lips, his chest, establishing no pattern, just marauding at will in a way that left him with no defenses at all.

He stripped away her jeans with sudden urgency, then assisted her in removing his own. He drew her close, pausing in the rapidly escalating tension to cherish the moment when their flesh caressed from head to toe, warm, exquisitely warm and gently provocative. Then Katie's leg draped over his thigh, thrusting her hips against his in a way that demanded an end to subtlety and innocence and a return to passion.

Excitement built to a feverish intensity as Katie gave herself to him, offering up her body, hips arching into his, seeking as she cried out his name, urging him to love her. Ross poised over her and gazed into her eyes, which were wide and bright and anxious.

"Now, Ross, please. Love me now."

He lowered himself gently, though he knew she

wanted a wild joining. He needed to show her that what began in gentleness and love could end in ecstasy and passion, a vision of their future. He filled her slowly, then retreated, then filled her again. Each time they came together, her eyes widened with surprise and delight, until there was no longer time for thought or reason or even understanding. There was only feeling, a spectacular, exquisite tension, followed by a rainbow's burst of color and a joyous release that tumbled them back from the heavens and left them both damp and tired and sated.

Katie wouldn't let Ross leave her. "Stay with me."

"I'm too heavy."

"No. I need to feel you. I need to know this was real and not just a glorious dream."

He kissed away the dampness on her cheek. Perspiration, or a tear? "Are you okay, Katie love?"

"I'm fine." She held on tighter.

She *was* fine. Terrific, in fact. Jennifer and Maggie had been right. Ross, she'd discovered, was everything she'd ever needed, everything she could possibly want. In his arms, she'd found the unexpected, felt unsurpassed excitement, gone beyond her wildest dreams. She'd experienced the act of love before, but in all her years of marriage she had never felt completed, never felt such vivid sensations, and not once had she known what it was to lose herself in such exquisite ecstasy. She'd been tempted by a fantasy, but fate had intervened and given her a more spectacular reality.

They made love again and again through the night, each time as new and fascinating and thrilling as the first. By morning, they had abandoned any thought of taking the ferry to Victoria. With breakfast and the paper spread around them, they spent Sunday morning feeding each other bits of scrambled egg and toast spread with orange marmalade, laughing over the comics, arguing about politics, and, finally, making love once more.

The memory of the wickedly pleasurable weekend carried Katie into the next week on a cloud. It should have lasted her forever.

But then the mail came.

CHAPTER NINE

Enchantress,

My love, suddenly I have so many doubts. Over the last few weeks, I feel I have gotten to know you through your refreshingly candid letters. You are an intriguing woman who could keep a man endlessly fascinated. Yet I sense an ambivalence in you that worries me. I fear I could be losing you. There's so much I'd like to tell you, but I must have a sign before I speak. If you are not committed to another, please meet me at the base of the Space Needle at six o'clock on Friday. Until then . . .

IT HAD BEEN RAINING for five straight days when the letter came. The sky was an endless, depressing gray, and the persistent fine mist created a chilling dampness that made the bones ache and the mind wander.

Katie's mind was far from Chandler Electronics even before the arrival of the mail. Her thoughts were in Los Angeles with Ross, who'd been away for three days, probably basking in the sun on the beach, she thought resentfully and unfairly. She knew perfectly well he was spending his time in business meetings. He'd called every night to tell her about his day, to ask about hers.

Ross apparently didn't believe in long-distance romance, however. The calls were brisk and businesslike and unsatisfying, not at all like having the same sort of conversation whispered across a pillow. And after only a few short weeks, she'd grown to count on those late-night talks, those stolen moments when Lisa was staying over with a friend and she and Ross could spend an entire night in each other's arms.

In the last week or so, though, he'd seemed increasingly distracted. He wasn't nearly as attentive as he had been when their romance was first heating up. She'd tried to probe for explanations, but he'd denied that anything had changed. Much as she hated the possibility, she wondered if he was one of those men whose interest waned as soon as the thrill of the chase ended.

As a result of the rotten weather and Ross's distant mood, Katie felt lonely and restless. She was ripe for something to break the monotony, to brighten her own mood. This latest letter was made to order. Her hand was actually shaking when she finished reading it. After several weeks of increasingly frequent correspondence, her mystery man wanted to meet her at last. Excitement surged through her, followed by

temptation, then hesitation. What should she do?
What the hell should she do?

She couldn't deny a strong desire to meet the author of the notes, the man who seemed to know her
so well and who had made such ardent declarations
of love without ever having met her. She wanted to
see for herself if he was as romantic, bold, and fascinating as he seemed. She wanted to know if he was
rich or poor, if he only dreamed of adventures or if
he made them happen. He'd asked so much of her,
but told her so little about himself in return. Her
curiosity, which had begun to abate in the warm af-
terglow of falling in love with Ross, was suddenly
killing her.

Curiosity killed the cat.

The familiar warning taunted her.

Satisfaction brought it back.

Would there be any satisfaction in knowing, or
only disappointment, an end to a fantasy?

And there was Ross to consider. He would be back
on Friday morning. How on earth would he react if
he knew she was going to meet another man after
their relationship had progressed into such a passionate intimacy? He'd been jealous enough when she'd
gone out to lunch with another man weeks ago, when
the two of them had been nothing more than business associates. There was no telling what he would
do if he found out about this.

She was less concerned about his jealousy, though,
than she was about hurting him. It was very likely he
would see this as a betrayal of some sort—even *she*
did—and yet they had made no commitments. Ross
had skirted that issue with the skillful maneuvering
of a career diplomat. No, she corrected, to be honest, he hadn't really avoided it. It simply hadn't come

up, which left her right where she'd started, filled
with uncertainty.

The internal debate kept her awake all night
Thursday and made her feel incredibly guilty when
Ross came into her office on Friday morning bearing
a present, a tiny gold unicorn pendant to remind her
of how she'd cried when they'd watched *The Glass
Menagerie* together on the late-night movie.

Throughout the day, guilt plagued her. Every time
Ross kissed her, she felt another twinge. She'd even
compounded her dilemma by convincing herself that
by not going she would be betraying this other man.
By refusing to meet him, it would seem as though
she'd just been leading him on. What an unbeliev-
able fix for a woman who'd had no men at all in her
life just a couple of months ago!

"Are you okay?" Ross finally asked, picking up on
her odd mood.

"Fine."

His penetrating gaze made her squirm uncomfort-
ably. "Are you sure there's not something you'd like
to talk about?" he probed.

She shook her head, then wondered at the shut-
tered look that came into his eyes as he shrugged and
walked away.

To go or not to go? The question taunted her all
day. Why *not* go? she decided finally. She and Ross
didn't have plans until later in the evening. She
could at least go to the Space Needle, meet the man,
and tell him that she was involved with someone
else. It would be the polite thing to do, sort of like
telling an old lover in person that the affair was
through. Afterward, she would tell Ross all about it.
There would be no betrayal.

Still, once the decision had been made, she

turned into a nervous wreck, jumping like a scared cat every time her intercom buzzed and she heard Ross's voice. She still felt like a traitor. Ross seemed oddly distracted as well, casting speculative glances in her direction throughout the endless afternoon. Those puzzled looks of his only added to the uneasy atmosphere around the office.

At five o'clock her plans, so carefully laid out, went completely haywire. Ross tore into her office, running his fingers through his dark hair in a gesture she'd come to recognize as the first sign of intense agitation.

"We've got problems," he announced, pacing to and fro in front of her desk.

"Problems?"

"Roger Simpson called. He's heard a rumor that Dorian Hayes might be ready to market a robot like Mr. Mom."

"What? Not again!" Katie was incredulous. If this sort of thing kept up, it could eventually wipe out Chandler Electronics and everything Ross had worked for.

"I know," he said, his tone edged with frustration. "I don't understand it, either. I thought we'd kept this thing completely under wraps. Who's seen the contracts besides that two of us?"

"Paula did the typing, but as far as I know she's the only one who's had any of the material. The rest of the time, it's been locked in my files."

"Well, someone else has seen it," Ross said, his voice shaking with restrained anger. "I hope to God I never get my hands on the person. I won't be responsible for my actions."

"Calm down," Katie soothed, though she felt a little like screaming herself. "This isn't the end of the world. We'll come up with a plan."

"All I know is we can't leave here tonight until we figure out who's behind this." He glanced at her and smiled ruefully. "It's my own fault, you know."

"How can you say that?"

"I've been so distracted with you lately that I've allowed myself to forget all about this threat from Hayes. He swore years ago to get even with me. It looks as though he's finally found a way to do it."

"Why does he hate you so much? How do you know him?"

"We met in college. We were both dating Jaclyn."

Katie's eyes widened. "But you said it had something to do with ethics."

"It did. He tried to win Jaclyn by lying to her about me. She found out what he'd done and married me. Now I have to wonder if she didn't marry me out of spite, simply because she was angry at him."

"Why on earth would you think that? Surely she must have loved you then."

Ross shook his head. "I thought so at the time. I really wanted to believe it, but she went back to Hayes when she left me."

"Oh, Ross, no," Katie whispered. "I had no idea."

"Interesting, the twists and turns betrayal can take, isn't it?"

It was the first time Katie had heard the bitterness, the first time Ross had allowed her to feel his pain, and it was all because of a woman's betrayal. She had to wonder if he would ever have forgiven her for what she'd been about to do this evening.

"It's not too late," Katie consoled, knowing only she was aware of the double meaning in her words. "We'll find the answers."

"At least maybe we can beat Hayes on the robot, if we act quickly. Simpson's on his way over, so we can sign the contract and get into production right away."

Katie suddenly frowned.

"What is it?" Ross asked.

"Is it possible that Simpson is making this up, just to force a decision on the deal?"

Ross stopped his pacing and stared at her. "I never thought of that." Then he shook his head. "If he'd mentioned anyone other than Hayes, I'd agree with you, but it's too much of a coincidence that he'd pick the one man who's been beating us all along."

"It can't be that much of a secret, though, that we've had problems with Hayes. We've scrapped a couple of projects in the early stages of production. Anyone could have given that information to Simpson. He might even know about Jaclyn."

"Damn. Does that mean we have one leak or two?"

"I don't know."

Ross sighed wearily. "We'll have to worry about that later. Let's go over the contract one last time, so we can have it ready when Simpson gets here."

Katie glanced at her watch. It was already five-thirty. There was no way she'd make it to the rendezvous, and it was probably just as well in light of what she'd discovered about Ross's past. With a soft sigh of regret and a contradictory sense of relief, she went to her files and got the Simpson folder.

Roger Simpson and his attorney arrived a few minutes later. Mercifully, they didn't have Mr. Mom in tow. Ross went through the changes in the contract with the two men.

"It looks fine to me," Simpson said. "I'm anxious to get into production."

"I'm sure you are," Katie said, avoiding Ross's quick glance of surprise. She kept her tone exceptionally casual. "How did you hear about the Dorian Hayes project?"

Simpson's expression was without guile. "You know it's a funny thing about that. Early on, we had approached them about Mr. Mom, and they weren't interested. A couple of days ago, I ran into one of their engineers in a bar, and we got to talking. He mentioned he'd been working on this robot, said he thought the whole thing was kind of crazy, but Hayes had put a rush on it about six weeks ago. When he'd asked him why, Hayes said he had a gut feeling robots were going to be big for the holiday season."

Katie and Ross exchanged glances. It had been exactly six weeks ago that they'd had their meeting with Simpson and Mr. Mom. Had someone related the outcome of that meeting to Dorian Hayes?

"But Hayes hadn't felt that way when you talked to him?" Ross said.

"Not even close. He'd practically laughed in my face, said the whole thing was impractical."

"Did the engineer have any idea what changed his mind?"

"No. He just shrugged and said he'd gotten used to that kind of craziness over there. He said he hadn't worked on a project yet that hadn't been a rush of some kind."

"I see," Ross said. "Thanks for the information. With any luck, we should be able to beat them on this."

"I think so. I don't think there's any way they could be past the preliminary stages. My plans are complete. It's just a matter of tooling up and going into production."

It was after seven by the time the deal had been signed, and Simpson and his attorney had left. Ross sank down in the chair across from Katie and leaned back. He closed his eyes.

"So," he said at last. "What do you think?"

"Well, I do have one idea, but it's pretty off the wall."

"I don't care. At this point I'll listen to anything."

"Dorian Hayes is in electronics, just like you."

Ross's brow quirked and he opened one eye disdainfully. "Okay. Now tell me something I don't know."

"Don't get nasty," she retorted. "I'm trying to build this in a logical way."

"Of course, " he said tolerantly. "It might be better, though, if you'd just blurt it out."

She glared at him. "Okay, then. Maybe he's bugged the place."

"Bugged the place?" Ross's tone rose incredulously. "Katie, were you watching those spy shows again while I was gone?"

"Go on. Make fun of me, but it isn't out of the realm of possibility. We haven't found a single bit of evidence to link any of our employees to the leaks, have we?"

"No, but maybe we just haven't dug deep enough."

"If we dig any deeper, we'll have to go through their parents' birth records."

"Okay, so you've been very thorough, but bugging? Please, Katie."

She leaned back in her chair. "Fine. You don't like my theory, come up with a better one."

"Dammit, I don't have a better one."

She grinned at him smugly and felt exactly as

though she'd been given an assignment to help James Bond. "Then it wouldn't hurt to get one of those devices that can sweep a place for bugs, would it?"

"I suppose you know where to find one, super sleuth."

Her face fell.

"I thought so," he said with an infuriatingly satisfied smirk.

"Okay," she grumbled. "What about the Yellow Pages?"

"And what would you like to look under?"

"Security systems," she retorted, snatching the phone book off the shelves behind her desk, flipping through the pages until she found what she wanted. She passed him the opened book. Several companies offered the type of service she felt they needed.

"I'll call first thing on Monday," Ross said, his expression subdued.

"This one has a twenty-four-hour hot line," she said, jabbing her finger at one of the ads. "I'll call now."

"It can wait over the weekend. There won't be anything going on around here anyway."

She grinned at him. "Maybe *it* can wait, but *I* can't."

For the first time all evening, Ross laughed. "Okay, okay. I'll call. If you're right, I'll take you out for champagne and caviar."

"If I'm right," she corrected softly, "you'll take me home with you."

Desire flared in Ross's eyes. "That, Katie love, goes without saying." His voice softened. "I've missed you."

"I've missed you, too." Another twinge of guilt nagged at her conscience. *Forget about it,* she told herself. *You didn't go to the meeting, so it's over. It doesn't matter.*

But it did.

"Ross, there's something we should talk about," she said finally, after he'd hung up from talking with the security company.

"Does it have anything to do with our problem here?"

"No."

"Then it'll have to wait. The security guy is on his way over. I want to take a look around before he gets here."

Katie sighed and tried to recapture some of her excitement at the prospect of unearthing a spying device. Suddenly the whole thing seemed silly. Obviously, she'd just gotten caught up in all this adventure and intrigue nonsense since she'd been writing to her mysterious stranger. The fact of the matter probably was that some disgruntled employee, who'd successfully masked his disaffection, was behind the leaks. In the corporate-espionage business it was probably far easier to buy a spy than it was to plant a bug. Ross was going to wring her neck when the expensive sweep turned up nothing.

An hour later, it had revealed two electronic listening devices, one in her office, another in his.

"Katie, you're a genius," Ross said, giving her a thoroughly unsatisfying peck on the cheek as he followed the security expert through the rest of the offices. There were no other bugs. Katie held one of the devices in her hand and tried to feel a stirring of excitement. All she felt was relief.

"Does this mean you'll stop teasing me about my vivid imagination?"

"Absolutely. Now I want you to put it to work on figuring out how they got in here."

"What does it matter? They've been removed. We're alerted to the possibility. We'll just have to be more careful about where we discuss sensitive material."

"I will not have an office in which I cannot discuss business."

"Then take out a contract with that security company, because you'll have to have that man here regularly. Think of him as your bug exterminator."

Ross glowered at her. "Bad pun."

"Sorry, I couldn't help it. That's what happens when I start starving to death. My mind goes." Her stomach rumbled for emphasis.

"Good heavens, it's nearly ten, and we missed dinner!"

"And lunch, you slave driver. You wanted to get caught up on everything you missed while you were in L.A.," she reminded him. "I think I'll take the champagne and caviar after all. I'll even take a Big Mac, if it's faster."

"Does that mean you've forgotten all about coming home with me?"

"Not for a minute. I sent Lisa to Jennifer's for the weekend."

In less than half an hour, they were at Ross's apartment, settled in front of the fire with a lavish spread of hamburgers, fries, and milk shakes. Hunger had won out over elegance. When Katie finished the last french fry, she leaned back against the sofa with a sigh.

"That's much better."

"You're sure you're not going to starve now?" Ross teased.

"Nope. Two cheeseburgers ought to hold me through the night."

"If they don't, the double order of fries will." He leaned back next to her, shifting so that their legs brushed and his fingers could rest on her thigh.

"What did you want to talk about earlier?"

Ross's question shocked Katie out of her contented lethargy. She'd forgotten all about the subject she'd intended to open up with him. It was probably best that it stay forgotten.

"It doesn't matter now. We can talk about it some other time. You must be exhausted."

"I'm not too tired to listen to you." He studied her and tried to figure out what had changed since he'd left her earlier in the week. She was as nervous as a teenager on a first date. The expression in her eyes was troubled, and right now she was chewing on her lower lip and studying the pile of his carpet. Since she'd expressed her dislike of that carpet more than once, he doubted if she'd suddenly found it fascinating.

"Come on, Katie. Get whatever it is off your chest."

"You're not going to like it."

"I figured that much out. Otherwise, you wouldn't be looking as though you were facing a date with an executioner."

She took a deep breath. "I had another one of those dates tonight," she finally blurted out as he just stared at her, his heart thudding to a stop as she rambled on nervously. "I mean, I didn't really go on it, because of what happened at the office, but I was going to go, and I wouldn't blame you for being furious."

"I see."

The words hung in the air. Katie squirmed.

"Go on. Say something," she finally muttered.

"I don't know what to say. I'm surprised, I guess. I've been thinking that what we have is pretty special."

Her wide blue eyes met his gaze, then faltered. "I think so, too."

"Then why were you going?"

"I'm not really sure."

"And this is one of the men who answered your ad?"

She nodded miserably. "I'm sorry. I feel like a rat. I know we haven't made any commitment, but all day I've felt like such a cheat."

"Katie, you have the right to date other men. You're right. We haven't made any commitment." It cost him the last vestiges of his sanity to get those words past lips gone suddenly dry. "You haven't dated a lot since your divorce. That's partly my fault. When you were ready, I did everything I could to stand in your way. If you feel the need to experiment, to see what's out there, I won't interfere the way I did before."

"You won't?"

"No."

"Oh." Her voice was flat, and she looked extremely uncomfortable. He wanted to touch her, but passion wouldn't solve this one. Katie had to reach her own conclusions about their relationship, and it was better if she did it with a cool head. Dammit.

"I guess I ought to go, then."

He sighed. "That's probably best. You need to think."

She got to her feet, and Ross followed her to the door. Every step was sheer torture.

She regarded him uneasily, and it nearly cost him his resolve. "Will I see you over the weekend?" she asked.

"Why don't we wait awhile? You think things through, and we'll get together next weekend and talk it all out."

"What about work? We'll see each other there, won't we?"

"No. I have to go back to Los Angeles on Monday anyway. It's all working out for the best. I want you to have whatever space you need."

He was being so blasted cool and reasonable, and it was costing him every bit of control he had. He wanted to shout at her, to tell her that no matter where she ran or whom she dated, she would never find anything better than what they had. Had they been together long enough for her to realize that? He wanted more time, but it was the one thing he didn't have. Those letters she'd been getting had forced the issue.

Instead of kissing her as he wanted to, he watched her go, feeling like a heel as she walked to her car with her head bent in dejection.

He'd seen the confusion in her eyes, heard the uncertainty in her voice. She was afraid, and he'd done that to her.

The next week was going to be hell, and it didn't help one earthly bit knowing that he was the one who'd made it that way. It was one thing to give Katie her freedom, to feel sure enough of their love to allow her to go. It was quite another to actually watch her walk away, not really knowing if she'd ever come back.

"Have faith," he murmured under his breath as

she drove away. "Trust her to find her way back."
He had faith.
He trusted her.
It was still hell.

CHAPTER TEN

Oh, sweet Enchantress,

What happened? Where were you on Friday night? I was so sure that you would be there, that you were the sort of woman who wouldn't be able to resist a chance to meet someone new, perhaps even to find a friend who shares your spontaneous zest for living. Your absence should be my answer, but I can't bear the thought of giving up so easily. Won't you please meet me just once? The Space Needle at six on Wednesday. I think we deserve one chance to see if the feelings we've shared on paper can develop into something real. After that, if you want me out of your life, I'll go. Think of how often you've told me how you fear boredom. Take this one risk. I promise you won't regret it.

THE LETTER LAY on Katie's desk, taunting her throughout the day. The guy knew exactly how to get to her with all this talk of boredom and taking risks. She'd never be able to forgive herself now, if she didn't go this one time. She'd always think of herself as a coward. She would always have regrets.

She even had Ross's blessing, which had frankly thrown her for a loop. She hadn't expected him to be quite so understanding. It had irritated the daylights out of her. She'd liked him a whole lot better when she'd known where she stood with him, when he'd been acting like an absolute bear every time some other man appeared on the scene.

On Tuesday night, in response to her SOS, Jennifer and Maggie both arrived on her doorstep within minutes of each other. They were breathless and wide-eyed.

"What on earth is the matter?" Jennifer demanded. "When you called, you sounded worse than you did the night Paul announced his departure."

"I feel worse," Katie said miserably. She handed the letter to Jennifer. "Read this."

"'Oh, sweet Enchantress—'"

"Not aloud. I can't take it."

"I don't blame you," Jennifer said. "Is this for real? What is it?"

"It's from that man I told you about."

"The one we told you to forget?" Maggie asked indignantly. "Obviously, you didn't listen to us."

"Not exactly," Katie admitted. "I should have, though. I feel as though I'm being torn in two."

Jennifer finished reading the letter, then handed it to Maggie. "You were actually going to meet this man on Friday night?" she said incredulously.

"Yes. I didn't go, though," she added defensively.

"I assume you came to your senses."

"I wish I could tell you that was it, but it wasn't. Ross and I got busy at the office. I couldn't get away."

"And that's the only reason you didn't go?" Maggie asked, not making any attempt to hide her dismay.

Jennifer was even less understanding. "What on earth possessed you? You have this wonderful man in love with you, and you want to go running off to have some tête-à-tête with a total stranger."

"I know, though I don't actually think of this man as a stranger anymore. I guess I was just feeling a little down, and going to see him seemed like it would be fun. It was something the old Katie would have done."

"May I remind you that the 'old' Katie was in high school? She wasn't a supposedly mature thirty-four-year-old who, as of a few days ago anyway, professed to being madly in love with another man. Has that changed?"

"No. Not really. I'm just not so sure how Ross feels."

"That's ridiculous," Jennifer replied. "Anyone can see that the man is head over heels in love with you. Even my dear, sweet husband, who's normally about as sensitive as a bulldozer to these things, picked up on it."

"Then why would Ross tell me to go out on dates if I wanted to?"

"He didn't!" Maggie's eyes were wide as saucers.

"He did."

"Exactly how did the subject of your dating come up?" she asked.

"I was feeling pretty guilty, and I confessed that I'd planned on meeting this guy, and Ross said it was fine with him."

Maggie and Jennifer exchanged worried glances. Watching them didn't do a lot to lift Katie's spirits.

"Sounds as though I blew it, doesn't it?"

"It sounds as though both of you could use a swift kick. You two are too old to be playing games."

"I'm not playing a game. I wanted to see this man just once. He was my fantasy. I was going to tell him it wouldn't work out, though. Ross is more than enough for me."

"Apparently, you didn't give *him* that impression."

"What now?" Maggie asked. "Are you going to see this guy tomorrow night?"

"I have to."

"You don't have to do anything," Jennifer retorted. "Face it, you want to. If you don't get this out of your system, you'll never be totally free to love Ross. You'll always wonder what you missed. I suspect Ross realized that, too. If you ask me, Ross Chandler is a hell of a guy."

"I know," Katie said with a sigh.

"I just hope you'll have sense enough to tell him that, the minute you finish with this absurd meeting tomorrow night."

Katie planned to do exactly that. She would meet this man, say hello and good-bye, then go to Ross, even if she had to catch a flight to L.A. and track him down at his hotel. She would tell him that she loved him, that she didn't want to date any other men, and then pray that it wasn't too late.

If you're so sure that Ross is the man you want, why are you even going to this meeting? a little voice nagged.

"Because . . . oh, hell, just because," she muttered, and slammed her fist into her pillow. "Because some fantasies just don't die. You have to kill them by taking a good long look at them in the light of day."

Wednesday, she decided as she tossed sleeplessly at three A.M., was going to be one hell of a day.

Ironically, for all her doubts about going to the meeting at the Space Needle, Katie found herself speeding home after work so she could change into something far more frivolous and feminine than the clothes she usually wore to the office. If this was to be her only meeting with a man with a romantic soul, she wanted to play her own role to the hilt. She wanted him to live with an image of her as he'd imagined her to be.

The clouds had broken late in the afternoon, and the early evening sky was clear, the air fresh and clean. It was going to be a lovely night, and the air seemed charged with electricity. Filled with expectation, her heart thudding against her ribs, Katie strolled through the park. Approaching the base of the Space Needle, the remnant from the World's Fair, she suddenly halted in her tracks. Her pulse skittered crazily, as confusion and anger and amazement spun through her mind so rapidly she couldn't settle on any one emotion.

There, pacing up and down not twenty feet away from her, was Ross. Damn the man! He was supposed to be in Los Angeles. She had talked to him half a dozen times during the day, and not once had he mentioned coming home.

For a moment she had the wild notion that he was here to meet someone else, but then he caught sight of her and a tentative smile played about his lips. The thought of fleeing careened through her mind, then vanished, replaced by a sudden fury that Ross, despite his promises of not interfering, was once again putting himself between her and another man. Guilt only added to her sense of outrage. In fact, if she hadn't felt so incredibly guilty, she might have acknowledged that the racing of her pulse had nothing to do with anger and everything to do with the thrill of seeing the man she loved when she'd least expected it. She wondered if she'd ever get over the little shivers that accosted her at the mere sight of the man.

For the moment, though, she concentrated on telling him just what she thought of his prying. It was something they were going to have to resolve, if they were to have any kind of a future together. Obviously, he'd found her letters and shown up here to check out the competition. Again.

She marched up the sidewalk and planted herself in front of him, ignoring the glimmer of warmth in his eyes and his welcoming smile.

"What brings you back from Los Angeles?" she asked calmly.

"I finished up there, and I wanted to get back."

"So you could spy on me?" she inquired coolly. Then all pretense of calm vanished. "How dare you. You were the one who told me to go ahead and date other men. You were the one who didn't seem to give a damn anymore how many men I went out with. So what gives you the right to pry into my private life again, to go through my correspondence and then follow me here? I'm sick of this, Ross Chandler. Do you realize I actually thought I was in love with you? How could I possibly love a man who doesn't trust me? How could I love a man who goes back on his word? How could I love a man who's so damned terrified of commitment that he simply wants to hang around with me and my daughter, instead of getting married and having a real family? I must have been out of my mind. You don't want me, but you don't want anyone else to have me, either. Well, you and all your insecurities and jealousy can go take a flying leap. I've had it. I'm glad I'm meeting someone new tonight. At least *he* seems to know what he wants."

Ross was silent, and she glared at him. "Now, just leave. I don't want you here when he comes," she said, finally winding down and noting that Ross's complexion had gone from ashen to red and was now edging toward an explosive shade of purple. Apparently, she'd overdone it just a little bit. The man appeared ready to kill. She edged backward. "Never mind. I'll just wait over there."

"Don't you move." Ross's softly spoken words cut through the air. Katie stopped in her tracks. "Look at me."

She glanced up, her eyes still flashing sparks.

"Are you quite sure you're through?" he asked. Suddenly, he seemed incredibly calm.

Katie's temper cooled, and her voice faltered. "I . . . I guess so."

"Be sure," he warned, "because I'm not up to another tirade."

"Okay, yes. I'm through."

"Now it's my turn."

"Ross, I don't want to hear your excuses."

"I didn't much want to listen to your wild accusations, but I did. Give me the same courtesy."

She glowered at him.

"For starters, I did not, as you're accusing me, go through your mail."

"Then how did you know where I'd be?" Her voice was laced with skepticism.

He gazed at her for what seemed to be an interminable length of time, allowing the tension to build, then said softly, "Because *I* wrote the letters."

The beat of Katie's heart slowed, then accelerated. She felt as though her wildest dream had suddenly become a reality, but such things didn't happen. Or did they?

"You?" she said incredulously, her eyes filling with wonder. A shock of insight flashed through her, and she knew it was true. Only Ross could have known her so well.

Then she thought about all the terrible things she'd just said to him and felt herself go pale. It was pretty amazing that he hadn't just turned around and walked away.

"I don't suppose you'd believe me if I told you I'd known all along," she suggested hopefully.

His lips twitched, then curved into a full-fledged grin. "Not a chance."

"I didn't think so," she said with an exaggerated sigh. "I'm sorry for yelling at you, but can you blame me?"

"I suppose not," he conceded reluctantly.

"I still don't understand why you'd send those letters, when we were already seeing each other."

"That's the tough one." He shrugged. "Caution. Maybe even fear."

"Fear? Of what?" Her expression was disbelieving. Ross wasn't afraid of anything.

"Well, you seemed to be more interested in finding a stranger to fall in love with than you were in dating me. At first, when you thought I had a hundred women on the string, you decided I was too wild for you. Then, when you found out I *wasn't* like that, that I enjoyed simple family life, it seemed to scare you even more. I decided I'd better hedge my bets. If I couldn't get you to fall for me, the guy writing the letters had another shot at it."

He was still standing far away from her, and she sensed his vulnerability. She could even begin to understand something of his uncertainty about her. While she'd been worrying about his making a commitment, he'd been watching her sort through potential dates like a woman going through fabric samples.

Katie sank down on a bench and gazed up at him. "I don't believe this."

"I'm not exactly positive about what's been going on for the last couple months myself. Who are you in love with? Me or the guy who wrote the letters?"

She grinned at him impishly, her heart thundering against her ribs at the realization that she wouldn't have to choose. She could have it all. Was it at all possible that on some level she *had* known? Probably not.

When she, Jennifer, and Maggie had written that ad, she had told them that no one man ever had all the qualities you were looking for, but she'd been wrong. Ross was exactly the man she'd been dreaming about. It wouldn't do to tell him that quite yet, though. He might have gone to a lot of trouble to show her how he felt, but he hadn't actually made any commitment. He hadn't said the words, and she needed to hear them.

"Who says I'm in love with anyone?" she inquired sweetly.

"Katie!"

"Since you're one and the same, it hardly seems relevant."

"You're avoiding the issue."

She nodded. "I certainly am."

"You are in love with one of us, though, aren't you?"

"Try me."

"Try you?" he repeated blankly.

"Ask me something. If you can't get it out of your mouth, I'll loan you a piece of paper."

Suddenly, Ross's eyes lit up, and he gave her a dazzling smile. "Oh, that!" he said, nodding in understanding. He sat down beside her on the bench and took her hand in his. A tingle of excited anticipation shot down her spine.

"Will you marry me, Katie Stewart?" he said solemnly.

"Which one of you?" she couldn't resist asking.

"Both of us."

"That's bigamy."

"Not in this case."

"Then, yes, I'll marry you, both of you, whatever."

"It does get confusing, doesn't it?" he said and kissed her, his lips warm and tender against hers, then hot and hungry and persuasive.

"Not when you do that. When you do that, everything is very clear."

"Then I must be doing something wrong. My kisses are supposed to make you dizzy."

"Let's try again," she suggested.

When they'd been trying for another ten minutes, she pulled away and whispered in Ross's ear.

"A ménage à trois?"

She grinned at him. "You started this," she reminded him. "I want to see if your romantic counterpart has any moves you don't."

"He doesn't," Ross said emphatically.

"How can you be so sure?" she teased. "Maybe you'll surprise yourself."

"I don't think so. If you ask me, the man's all talk."

"But such lovely talk," she murmured as they walked away arm in arm.

Much, much later, they were sitting in front of a blazing fire in Ross's apartment. He studied the contented, sleepy expression on her face. "Tell the truth, Katie love. Which of us are you in love with?"

She sighed. "You, I think."

"You think!" he said indignantly. "That's a hell of a note. You're going to marry me, but you only *think* you're in love with me!"

"I *am* in love with you," she said with certainty. "I'm in love with your down-to-earth lifestyle, your humor, the way you make me feel inside. I'm just not used to it yet. You're so different from what I expected. I thought all these things we've been doing the last couple of months would bore a man like you, that sooner or later you'd want to go back to your carefree ways."

"No," he said. "Remember, I've been reading all those letters of yours about jetting around the world and playing spy. I think the real point is that *you* thought all these simple things would bore *you*."

She considered what he said and saw some truth in it. "There you go again, reading my mind," she said, drumming her fingers nervously.

"I didn't have to read your mind, I just read between the lines. Your letters told me so much about you," he said, and she heard an oddly wistful note in his voice. "Sometimes I had to wonder if I was dealing with a split personality. Why wouldn't you share any of those dreams of yours with me? How come you could only write them to a man you thought you didn't know?"

"I guess at first I was afraid you'd laugh at me. Old down-to-earth Katie wanting to do such crazy, unpredictable things. Then, when I saw how much you seemed to like me the way I was, I thought it would turn you off, that you'd never want to share any of those dreams with me."

"Katie love, there is a part of me that's just as adventurous as you are and, even if there weren't, I'd want to share all your dreams. If you want to climb a mountain, we'll go, even if I get altitude sickness. I've already helped you turn into a detective, haven't I? We can make all of your dreams come true."

"Thank you," she said simply, her eyes shining. "You can't even begin to imagine what it means to me to have you say that. Even if we never go anywhere or do anything wild, I'll love you always just for offering."

"It was more than just an offer. We'll do it all," he promised. "First, though, there are some things we haven't talked about."

"What?"

"Do you want to go on working?"

Her eyes immediately clouded over, shadowed by doubts. "Of course. Don't you want me to?"

"Speaking as your boss, absolutely."

"And as my husband-to-be?"

"I want you to do whatever makes you happy. I just want you to be sure you're doing it for the right reasons."

"I don't understand."

"When you were married before, Paul didn't want you working, right?"

"Yes."

"Which made the idea of working all the more attractive."

"I'm beginning to catch on. You're saying this is just another one of my rebellions."

"No, I'm asking if it is. If you want to work, that's fine. If you want to work with me, that's even better. But you don't have to prove anything anymore, not to yourself and certainly not to me."

"I want to work. I love sharing in that part of your life and I like using my brain. Maybe later when we—"

Then he was grinning, firelight making his brown eyes spark like amber. "When we what?"

"We haven't talked about it. Do you want children?"

"We have Lisa."

"But she's not yours."

"She will be in every way that matters. I may not replace Paul for her, but I already love her just as much as any father could a child of his own."

"Then you don't want a baby?" Her voice was laced with disappointment.

"Oh, Katie love," he breathed softly, his lips touching hers oh so gently. "Of course I do. I can't imagine anything any more wonderful than a child that you and I would have together. He'd probably become president."

"*She* might even be a government agent."

"Or a mountain climber."

"Of course, you could have an ulterior motive here."

"What?"

"A baby would mean we wouldn't be able to go on those wild, adventurous trips your alter-ego promised me, at least not for a while."

"Will you mind?"

"Actually, I have a nagging little feeling that the fantasy of going on a safari or riding the rapids appealed to me more than the reality would."

He gave a heartfelt sigh of relief. "Thank God."

She slipped her arms around his waist and trailed kisses down his bare chest. "What would you have done if I'd said I was going to hold you to those promises?"

"Prayed a lot."

"Your prayers have been answered."

"They were answered the day you walked into my office."

"It took you long enough to realize it."

"And I suppose you knew from the first?"

"Actually I think maybe I did, but it wasn't until about three hours ago, when I saw you standing there at the Space Needle, that I dared to admit it to myself."

"And here I thought you were furious."

"I was."

"Oh."

"I was also very, very glad. The whole time I was yelling at you, what I really wanted to do was rush into your arms so you could hold me. I'd been so scared that you didn't care about my dating anymore, that it didn't matter to you."

"Oh, I cared. I just had to let you go for a while." His gaze was intent. "Are you sure I'm going to be exciting enough for you?" His hands began to rove again, caressing, probing until Katie was quivering.

"There's not a doubt in my mind," she said breathlessly as Ross's lips met hers and drew her back into the fantasy.

EPILOGUE

Happy anniversary, Enchantress!

It's been quite a year, hasn't it? Not many people our age spend their honeymoon learning to windsurf. I must confess that my arm hardly hurts a bit anymore. The doctor who set it must have known what he was doing. No matter what you think, though, I don't think we'll be ready for the next Summer Olympics. It might be best if we just watched them on TV. We wouldn't want to embarrass Lisa, anyway.

By the way, Enchantress, I want to thank you again for devising that ingenious scheme to get even with Dorian Hayes by feeding him false information about our production plans. I hear half of his engineers quit when he started asking them to work on short-range toy missiles.

And speaking of our old competition with Dorian Hayes, I was thinking of giving you Mr. Mom as an anniversary present, but I thought better of it. I was afraid you'd tell him to take over for you in the bedroom, too, just to make a point. Guess I'll have to save him for Lisa's birthday. Perhaps he could clean up her room so we can find out if the missing volumes of the encyclopedia are buried under her clothes.

Life with you, Enchantress, has been everything I imagined it could be, though I must admit I was a little surprised when you had the hot tub installed as a Christmas present. I'd never been able to imagine why anyone would want one of those things, until you showed me. Amazing! It was a New Year's Eve I'll never forget.

As for forgetting, do you realize that this was the first year since I was old enough to say "football" that I missed watching a Super Bowl? Offering to give me a massage fifteen minutes before the game was due to start was a dirty trick. You could have read a book, if you didn't want to watch the game with me.

I also owe you one for suggesting we go to Colorado on our vacation last summer. I had no idea, when I told you to make the arrangements, that we'd end up on a dude ranch. I doubt if I'll ever recover from walking around the corner of the house just in time to see that huge stallion throw you in the air. What on earth possessed you to get on that beast? You could tell by looking into his eyes that he couldn't be tamed, but then you always did like a challenge. That's why I fell in love with you. Just promise me you'll never ask me to ride a burro down into the Grand Canyon again.

What would you like to do on our anniversary? I know what you're thinking, but besides that. We should do something truly special this year, since by next year we'll be pretty well tied down with the baby. How about flying to Paris for dinner? Think our baby'd like that? Maybe he'd even pick up a little French. I've read that book you gave me. It says babies can learn a lot prenatally.

Our baby! I still can't quite get over it, Enchantress. The next few months can't possibly pass quickly enough. I'm going to be one of those disgustingly proud fathers who carries around a wallet full of pictures and bores everyone to death with the latest adventures of the baby.

There will be adventures, Katie love, a whole lifetime of them. We're just getting started.

SECOND CHANCE AT LOVE

COMING NEXT MONTH

A LADY'S CHOICE #432
by Cait Logan
Emily Northrup returns to her
rural hometown to nurse an ailing aunt
and clashes with her aunt's sexy neighbor,
Cal McDonald. Cal's fascinated Emily
since her teen-age years, and their passion
explodes as the townspeople place
bets on their wedding date…

CLOSE SCRUTINY #433
by Pat Dalton
F.B.I. agent Niera Pascotti
has lived dangerously while loving
cautiously—until a mandatory vacation
to Tahiti throws her into the arms of
mysterious Cort Tucker. Niera can't resist
Cort, yet she must discover his identity
while masking her own…

Second Chance at Love

Be Sure to Read These New Releases!

ANGEL ON MY SHOULDER #428
by Jackie Leigh

Angel Faye Darnell has fled fame and
fortune as a glitzy country singer to live
quietly incognito in the Rockies. But
sexy mountain man Gus Cougar changes
her plans, making Angel's new life more
dramatic—and passionate—than ever!

RULES OF THE HEART #429
by Samantha Quinn

Natasha O'Reilly is a fiery, funny
Bohemian, and William St. James is a
wealthy, proper entrepreneur. But these
opposites attract like fire to kindling,
and when Natasha moves into his house
to renovate it, their reservations are
stripped away with the wallpaper…

SECOND CHANCE AT LOVE

___ 0-425-10048-0	IN NAME ONLY #400 Mary Modean	$2.25
___ 0-425-10049-9	RECLAIM THE DREAM #401 Liz Grady	$2.25
___ 0-425-10050-2	CAROLINA MOON #402 Joan Darling	$2.25
___ 0-425-10051-0	THE WEDDING BELLE #403 Diana Morgan	$2.25
___ 0-425-10052-9	COURTING TROUBLE #404 Laine Allen	$2.25
___ 0-425-10053-7	EVERYBODY'S HERO #405 Jan Mathews	$2.25
___ 0-425-10080-4	CONSPIRACY OF HEARTS #406 Pat Dalton	$2.25
___ 0-425-10081-2	HEAT WAVE #407 Lee Williams	$2.25
___ 0-425-10082-0	TEMPORARY ANGEL #408 Courtney Ryan	$2.25
___ 0-425-10083-9	HERO AT LARGE #409 Steffie Hall	$2.25
___ 0-425-10084-7	CHASING RAINBOWS #410 Carole Buck	$2.25
___ 0-425-10085-5	PRIMITIVE GLORY #411 Cass McAndrew	$2.25
___ 0-425-10225-4	TWO'S COMPANY #412 Sherryl Woods	$2.25
___ 0-425-10226-2	WINTER FLAME #413 Kelly Adams	$2.25
___ 0-425-10227-0	A SWEET TALKIN' MAN #414 Jackie Leigh	$2.25
___ 0-425-10228-9	TOUCH OF MIDNIGHT #415 Kerry Price	$2.25
___ 0-425-10229-7	HART'S DESIRE #416 Linda Raye	$2.25
___ 0-425-10230-0	A FAMILY AFFAIR #417 Cindy Victor	$2.25
___ 0-425-10513-X	CUPID'S CAMPAIGN #418 Kate Gilbert	$2.50
___ 0-425-10514-8	GAMBLER'S LADY #419 Cait Logan	$2.50
___ 0-425-10515-6	ACCENT ON DESIRE #420 Christa Merlin	$2.50
___ 0-425-10516-4	YOUNG AT HEART #421 Jackie Leigh	$2.50
___ 0-425-10517-2	STRANGER FROM THE PAST #422 Jan Mathews	$2.50
___ 0-425-10518-0	HEAVEN SENT #423 Jamisan Whitney	$2.50
___ 0-425-10530-X	ALL THAT JAZZ #424 Carole Buck	$2.50
___ 0-425-10531-8	IT STARTED WITH A KISS #425 Kit Windham	$2.50
___ 0-425-10558-X	ONE FROM THE HEART #426 Cinda Richards	$2.50
___ 0-425-10559-8	NIGHTS IN SHINING SPLENDOR #427 Christina Dair	$2.50
___ 0-425-10560-1	ANGEL ON MY SHOULDER #428 Jackie Leigh	$2.50
___ 0-425-10561-X	RULES OF THE HEART #429 Samantha Quinn	$2.50
___ 0-425-10604-7	PRINCE CHARMING REPLIES #430 Sherryl Woods	$2.50
___ 0-425-10605-5	DESIRE'S DESTINY #431 Jamisan Whitney	$2.50
___ 0-425-10680-2	A LADY'S CHOICE #432 Cait Logan	$2.50
___ 0-425-10681-0	CLOSE SCRUTINY #433 Pat Dalton	$2.50
___ 0-425-10682-9	SURRENDER THE DAWN #434 Jan Mathews (On sale Mar. '88)	$2.50
___ 0-425-10683-7	A WARM DECEMBER #435 Jacqueline Topaz (On sale Mar. '88)	$2.50
___ 0-425-10708-6	RAINBOW'S END #436 Carole Buck (On sale Apr. '88)	$2.50
___ 0-425-10709-4	TEMPTRESS #437 Linda Raye (On sale Apr. '88)	$2.50

Available at your local bookstore or return this form to:

SECOND CHANCE AT LOVE
THE BERKLEY PUBLISHING GROUP, Dept. B
390 Murray Hill Parkway, East Rutherford, NJ 07073

Please send me the titles checked above. I enclose _____. Include $1.00 for postage and handling if one book is ordered; add 25¢ per book for two or more not to exceed $1.75. CA, NJ, NY and PA residents please add sales tax. Prices subject to change without notice and may be higher in Canada. Do not send cash.

NAME _____

ADDRESS _____

CITY _____ STATE/ZIP _____

(Allow six weeks for delivery.)